FRANCES

W.D.VALGARDSON

Frances

A Groundwood Book

DOUGLAS & McINTYRE

TORONTO VANCOUVER BUFFALO

Groundwood Books/Douglas & McIntyre
720 Bathurst Street, Ste. 500, Toronto, Ontario M5S 2R4

Distributed in the USA by Publishers Group West
1700 Fourth Street, Berkeley, CA 94710

We acknowledge the financial support of the Canada Council for the Arts, the Ontario Arts Council and the Government of Canada through the Book Publishing Industry Development Program for our publishing activities.

Canadian Cataloguing in Publication Data
Valgardson, W.D.
Frances
1st ed.
"A Groundwood book".
ISBN 0-88899-386-2 (bound) ISBN 0-88899-397-8 (pbk.)
I. Title.
PS8593.A53F62 2000   jC813'.54   C00-930563-7
PZ7.A53Fr 2000

Design by Michael Solomon
Cover art by Julia Bell
Printed and bound in Canada

For my granddaughter, Holly

1

‏··‏
‏··‏

Frances was pulling a piece of wool off a thorn bush when suddenly she heard someone laugh. She turned, expecting to see her grandmother.

No one was there. Just the old barn and, behind it, the remains of the log house where her great-great-grandmother and great-great-grandfather had lived. The roof on the log house had caved in many decades before. Now poplar trees grew inside the walls.

When Frances was younger, this had been her own private forest. She would put out a towel for a table-cloth, then set out her dishes and pour lemonade from her thermos. She always had a plate of choco-late chip cookies. Her friends liked those best.

"My friends live there," she'd told her mother. "They like lemonade."

Her friends were a group of boys, all about the same age. They explored the bush behind the farm looking for rabbits. They climbed trees to look at birds' eggs. They took a picnic lunch to eat on the edge of the field when they were searching out wildflowers. Sometimes they had great adventures, taking on whatever roles Frances chose for them.

Her mother had snapped her lips in that disapproving way she had. She didn't believe in magical friends. She had no time for that sort of stuff. Pretend friends didn't help her sell real estate. Hard work was what bought groceries and paid the taxes.

Frances's gran, though, had winked and smiled. Her gran was the kind of person who, when Frances was little, made sure the tooth fairy left some money under her pillow. When Frances was afraid of the dark, Gran was the one who elaborately checked under her bed and in her closet to make sure there were no monsters hiding there. Her mother bought her a nightlight.

"Frances, quit lollygagging," her mother yelled.

Lollygagging was her mother's favorite word. She was against lollygagging. She was against most things except studying or washing the dishes or polishing the van.

When Frances was six, her mother had given her lessons on how to answer the phone and take messages properly. Nowadays, her mother never went anywhere without her cellular. They might be in the midst of roasting wieners and the cellular would ring and her mother would be off like a shot, leaving her wiener to char.

"You should have a phone transplanted into your ear," Gran had said. "They're doing that now, I hear."

Her mother had winced. She was always wincing at Gran's remarks, but if it weren't for Gran babysitting and making meals and doing laundry, Emily—that was Frances's mother—wouldn't have been able to dash away and dazzle people into buying houses and cottages.

She also had a rule against being called Mom.

"Emily is a perfectly good name," she'd said to Frances. "I don't want to be defined by the fact that I gave birth. I am a person, not a thing." She also didn't want Frances calling her grandmother Amma. She wanted her to use Fjola, but her grandmother put her foot down. They had a fight and finally compromised on Frances being able to call her Gran.

Frances rolled the bit of wool between her fingers. A sheep had rubbed against the thorn bush. A little bit of wool, she thought. She was going to throw it away, then changed her mind and dropped it into her pocket. That was one of her habits that distressed her mother to no end—collecting useless odds and ends of things.

Right now they were supposed to be seeing if there was anything valuable in the old barn. Her great-amma and afi had stored all sorts of things there. Farm-equipment things. Most of it was rusted or broken.

"Better us than some tourist going by," her mother said. She'd never wanted to have anything to do with the old farm, but one of her clients who was into antiques had told her how the countryside was filled with abandoned buildings that held items worth a veritable fortune.

Veritable, Frances thought, was a wonderful word. She liked words like that. Old-fashioned words. Words with more than one syllable. Bumptious was a good word. And serendipity. She had to be careful around other kids, though, not to use too many of them. If she did, they thought she was putting on airs. But she wasn't, really. She just liked to roll words around in her mouth like smooth stones. Her mother blamed it on her grandfather. He'd taught her to say *Islindingadagurinn* before she was five.

"Crippled her mind for life," her mother once said to Aunt Martha. Her mother thought long words had a debilitating effect on small minds. She thought words should be like pants. Short pants for short legs, long pants for long legs. Short words for....

"Frances," her mother yelled. "We need you."

Frances recognized that sound. She'd lollygagged enough. She rushed to the barn.

"We need you to go into the loft. Your great-grand-father was always chucking stuff up there. Who knows what those men might have put up there and forgotten."

"It might be better if some things were left alone," Gran said. "Sometimes it doesn't pay to stir things up. I thought you didn't want anything to do with all that old stuff."

"Money changes people's minds," her mother said. "Old things are going for outrageous prices. That's what Sybil told me and she's an interior decorator. She even buys old barns just for the boards. Takes them apart piece by piece."

There was a wooden ladder nailed to the wall. Frances looked up. Above the ladder was a square hole.

"Just hop up there, Frances," her mother said. "I'd do it myself but you're younger than me." She always said it as if there was the possibility that one day Frances might be older than her.

The ladder creaked. The rungs were worn smooth with climbing. Frances poked her head through the hole, then sneezed. There were a lot of spider webs and dust. It looked like there were bits of this and that strewn about. She scrambled up, then tested the boards with her foot. She didn't want to go crashing through them.

There was some rotted canvas that smelled musty. She threw it out the loft door. There were bits and pieces of metal she didn't recognize. None of them looked like antiques. They looked more like the car parts her uncle Ben always had lying about the garage. Except these were much bigger. A lot of them were old rusted gears. She doubted her mother would want to decorate their cottage with gears, but she chucked those down, too. The best way to rummage was to clear everything out. Then you were sure you weren't missing anything.

"There's an old chair without a seat," she yelled. It was small and green and had short legs. It looked like it was for a child or a very, very tiny adult.

Her mother wanted to see it so Frances handed it down the hole.

There were some overalls that the rats had turned into a nest. They were all chewed to pieces. She threw those out. There was a lot of wire in rolls. A tractor seat. A wooden bar with two metal pieces in the shape of a U. She handed that down.

"That was for the oxen," her gran explained.

"Oxen!" Frances exclaimed. She didn't know the family ever had oxen. She'd only ever seen pictures of them. Big brutes. Bigger than the cows on Joe Finbogasson's farm.

She found a dishpan that had a hole in it. She

threw it out. Then she found a treasure. An oil lamp with its chimney unbroken. She carried it to the hole. Her mother was so happy that she even climbed up the ladder to get it. It was covered in dust and her mother hated dust. She talked about dust the way other people talked about vile criminals. She loved the lamp so much that she never mentioned the dust.

In the farthest corner, Frances found a wooden box. She couldn't get the lid open. It had rope handles. She dragged it across the floor. The box was so heavy that she could only pull it a bit at a time. She braced her feet and pulled backwards with all her might. The box jerked forward. She stepped back, got a good grip and jerked it again.

"Frances!" her mother yelled.

Frances knew that yell. It meant, "What are you up to, Frances? Are you lollygagging about? Are you doing something that you shouldn't be doing and if you are you're in big trouble."

When Frances was two, she'd been caught floating her plastic boats in the toilet. Since then her mother was convinced that she had to be watched every moment of every day. She believed in portents, and playing with boats in the toilet, even though it was sanitized with bleach three times a day, was a portent of worse to come.

Portent, Frances thought happily to herself. She hoped her life would be full of portents.

She pulled and grunted. Grunted and pulled. She knew they could hear her. Her mother was in so much expectation that something truly valuable had been found that she never made any comments about pigs grunting.

"What is it?" Gran asked when Frances leaned over the hole. She sounded worried.

"A box," Frances answered. "Full of something. I'm going to need help getting it down."

Her mother climbed up to have a look. She stood on the ladder with her head through the hole.

"It's old," she said, letting go with one hand and rubbing the top of the box. "Eighteen seventy-three, Fjola! It's a real antique. Can't you get the lid open, Frances?"

"I've tried, but it won't budge."

"We need a piece of rope. We could lower it."

"Emily, we could get Ben to help us the next time he comes to visit," Gran said.

"Nonsense," Emily replied. "We don't need any man to help us. We're liberated." But Frances knew it wasn't a matter of being liberated. If there was something valuable in the box, her mother wasn't going to want to share it with Uncle Ben and Aunt Martha.

"Some things should just be left alone," Gran said.

"No need to drag stuff out of the past. Done's done. There are lots of nice new things. You can get one of those beautiful cedar trunks that Joe makes."

Frances nearly scratched her head in wonderment. Her mother was always saying forget yesterday, it's over, live for today and tomorrow, get on with your life, you can't change the past—stuff like that. Her grandmother, on the other hand, was always wanting to preserve pieces of the past like the old post office and the railway station.

Now here they were on opposite sides of the argument, just like they'd traded personalities.

"It's so heavy, you'd think it was filled with gold," Emily said.

"Lead weights from the nets, more likely," Gran retorted. Their voices floated up into the hayloft from below. "There are some things better left alone, Emily. You start something and you never know where it might end."

2

They went back the next day with a rope. Frances and her mother managed to get the rope around the trunk. Then they let it down through the hayloft door.

"Don't stand underneath it, Fjola," Emily yelled. "If the rope breaks, it'll squash you like a bug."

The rope didn't break. The trunk was on the ground when her mother realized they couldn't possibly lift it into the car. They decided to borrow a truck. That meant driving to the cottage, phoning a half dozen people before finding one with an available truck, then driving back out to the farm. That took a good two hours.

Emily was beginning to look a little undone. Not big undone. She would never look big undone, like blouse buttons torn off, skirt falling down, face covered in mud, one shoe lost. But she did look a little undone. Her blouse was untucked on one side and her hair, which usually was frozen into place by gallons of gel, had fallen over a bit, sort of like a house that had collapsed on one wall. There was a streak of dirt across her nose.

The Treasure of the Sierra Madre, Frances thought. When she thought about greed, she always thought about TTSM. A lot of people went searching for gold. Then, after they found it, they killed each other. TTSM would start after her mother got the trunk home. Once it was cleaned up and sitting impressively before the fireplace, her aunt and uncle would come over with some of the cousins and see it filled with bars of gold. That's when TTSM would begin. They'd all kill each other around the leather chesterfield. There would be bodies everywhere, and Frances would be left to call 911 and then go on TV to tell the story of their tragedy.

Cousin Fusi, a third cousin twice removed or, as her mother called him, the Local Yokel, came with his truck. He now departed with twenty dollars. He was so happy that he kept snapping his false teeth in and out.

"Any time you want moving things, you just call me," he said, rubbing the twenty between his thumb and forefinger. But Emily didn't encourage him. Her hair had collapsed a bit more and her skirt was sort of twisted from all the pushing and heaving. She would, Frances knew, have a complete nervous breakdown when she saw herself in the mirror and would have to have a cocktail in her Royal Albert tea cup. Cheaper than Valium, she always said, with fewer side effects.

The trunk sat in the middle of the living room on newspapers her mother had spread out to keep the dust off her carpets. They tried to force the lid open but no matter how they pulled or pried, it stayed stubbornly shut.

"There must be a way," Emily said. "There's no lock and no place to put a lock so the lock must be in the box itself."

They wiped the box, getting every speck of dust and cobweb off it. Then they studied it from every direction.

It wasn't a particularly beautiful box. It was longer than it was wide. It had a slightly rounded top. There were two ribs in the top. The sides were roughly carved with horses.

"Interesting carvings," Gran said. "They show the integrity of the carver. There's no concern for the marketplace."

"Folk art is in," Emily replied. "Hand-crafted. It should be worth quite a lot."

Frances ran her fingers lightly over the horses. They were wonderful. No details, just the outline of horses running freely like unfettered spirits. The numbers, 1873, were not, as they'd first thought, part of the lid, but each number was fixed in place with a single brass bolt. The trunk had been painted blue and the numbers red. Now most of the paint had faded away.

"We'll have another look at it in the morning," Emily finally said. "I need to put myself together."

Frances woke up while it was still dark. She looked at her bedside clock. Four A.M. She lay in bed and listened to the waves on the beach. That was one of the best things about the cottage. She loved going to sleep to the sound of the waves and waking up to the sound of the waves.

As she lay there, she could see the box, just as if it was sitting in front of her except that she was staring at the ceiling. She turned it around in her head, the way she could turn pictures of objects around on the computer.

There was a mystery to it, and she loved mysteries. When she grew up, she thought she might be a detective or a coroner or an anthropologist—someone who was always trying to find answers.

"Why do you want to know the answers to everything?" her mother often chided her.

"I don't know," Frances replied. "I just do. Questions need to be answered. Jars should have pickles or jam."

Her mother thought it was all nonsense. The only

thing she wanted to know was who wanted to sell a house and who wanted to buy one.

Frances slipped out of bed and crept into the living room. To her surprise, her gran was sitting there staring at the box. Frances sat down on the floor beside her.

"This was my gran's," Fjola whispered. "I'd forgotten all about it. The last time I saw it must have been when I was your age."

"My great-great-grandmother's," Frances said. She leaned forward and put her arms around the front of the box as if she were hugging it.

"She brought it out from Iceland with her. Imagine being thirteen and putting all your worldly goods in a box and then getting on a boat and traveling half the world to start a new life."

"There was the smallpox," Frances said. She'd heard that story. About everybody dying of smallpox.

"That was before," Gran said. "She didn't come out with the first settlers. The smallpox had come and gone and there was a settlement and some farms. There'd been flooding and terrible weather. A lot of the first settlers went to the Dakotas. Her father and aunt took over an abandoned farmstead."

They sat there in silence, listening to the waves, but Frances wasn't really hearing the water lapping on the shore. She was staring at the box, turning it this way and that in her mind.

She leaned forward, put her hand on the first number and twisted. She felt it give a little. She turned it harder and it stiffly moved to an angle. Then she did the same with the other three numbers.

This time when they pulled on the lid, it came up easily.

♦

"Books," her mother said in the morning. "We went to all that trouble to bring home a bunch of books." She picked one up and made a face at its mustiness. She opened it. "We can't even read them. They're in Icelandic." She held the book out at arm's length.

"That's poetry," Frances said. "You can tell from the way it's divided up."

"I should have known. Your great-grandfather was always reading. He could recite poetry all night long and sometimes he did."

"What'll we do with them?"

"Throw them out. Or give them to the old folks' home. I don't want them cluttering up the cottage. Besides, they probably have mites. They could end up making us all sick with mold and bugs and who knows what."

Frances wasn't having any of that. She'd found the box and she'd figured out how to open it. When you found a treasure, you didn't just throw it away.

She lugged the books into her bedroom. She lined

them up. She had hoped she might be able to read some of the words.

"You could have taught me Icelandic," she said to her mother as they were eating breakfast.

"I don't know any. Besides, I'm not interested in all this ethnic stuff. We're in Canada. Nostalgia for the past is a waste of time. I don't want to hear about Iceland. If it was so great, why did our family leave?"

"Gran says you spoke Icelandic when you were a kid. You even took lessons."

"I've forgotten it. I don't remember a single word. It's an uncouth language."

"You know some Icelandic, Frances," her gran said.

"Me?"

"Ponnukokur."

"That's Icelandic? I just thought that was another word for pancakes."

"Rullupylsa."

"Yuck." She'd tried to eat the circles of meat and fat on brown bread. She'd even tried with her eyes closed, pretending it was something she liked, like sliced ham with mustard and pickles. She couldn't get her teeth to open.

"You could have taught me Icelandic. I'll bet they've got great words."

"You can lead a horse to water," her gran replied.

"Your great-aunt Simmie read to you every night in Icelandic. She even had you saying the words after her. After you started school, you came home and said you didn't want to talk like that anymore because the kids made fun of your accent."

Frances knew her gran was right. She remembered repeating words after GAS (she'd thought it was hilarious that her aunt's initials spelled a word, especially since she was always complaining about having to burp) and reciting the alphabet. Then Simmie moved to Toronto. Now she was just a voice on the phone and a birthday card with five dollars in it.

Frances also remembered the disapproving look on her mother's face.

"A, B, C is good enough for me," she'd said. It was hard to learn something when you knew your mother didn't want you to learn it, especially when there were TV shows you wanted to watch.

Her mother cleaned up the chest and set it in front of the fireplace. Frances had to admit it looked pretty good. The lamp they'd found was on small table beside the window.

Frances had her hand in her pocket. She felt something. It was the bit of wool she'd pulled off the thorn bush.

The moment she had the wool in her hand, she felt strange. Not dizzy, exactly, but sort of floating, like her body wasn't quite settled on the ground.

"What's the matter?" her mother asked.

"Nothing," Frances said.

"Don't you go acting strange on me. Keep your eyes focused on what's important. The bottom line."

"Born under the glacier," Gran said.

"Fjola!" Frances's mother exclaimed. "Don't start that."

Gran looked out the window, across the marsh. Frances could hear the red-winged blackbirds mewing in the bulrushes. The water was silver-blue all the way to the tree line. It was a long way across. One day Frances hoped to paddle a canoe from the east shore to the west and back again, but her mom wouldn't allow it yet. The wind could come up all of a sudden and the lagoon got real choppy. She wasn't to go more than fifty feet from shore. If the canoe went over, she could swim fifty feet.

Before she and her gran went for a walk, Frances heard her mother say, "Don't be filling her head with silly ideas."

They walked toward the point where the sandbar turned into marsh. The sand was hot and dusty. The frogs were quiet. Frances knew they were there in the grass along the roadside, but they'd be hunkered down in the shade. Big leopard frogs. The kind some people caught and killed so they could eat their legs.

She caught them just so she could hold them. When they realized she wasn't going to hurt them, they calmed down and settled into her hands. After she'd held them a bit, she always slipped them back into the grass or eased them into the water.

"What was that about glaciers?" she asked.

"Oh, nothing," her gran replied, but Frances knew that if she just kept quiet and didn't press the question, her gran would tell her.

After they'd walked a bit, her gran said, "Our people come from Snaefellsness. That's a district in Iceland. There's a large glacier there and people born there are said to be born in the shadow of the glacier."

"Like being born on the shores of Lake Winnipeg?"

"Yes."

Frances didn't quite believe it. If that was all it was, then why had her mother been so sharp about not filling her head with nonsense.

I have, she thought, the strangest family. There were all these secrets or, at least, she thought there were secrets. Something would come up and everybody would quit talking or someone would change the subject or they'd look at each other like they all knew something she didn't. A conspiracy of dunces or something.

"I'd like to see where we came from. Why can't I go with you to Iceland next month?"

"There may not be time to visit the old farm. Besides, it's been forty years since I visited last. The people who live there now may not want visitors."

"Snaefellsness," Frances said. "What's it like?"

"Ocean in front, mountains behind. Home fields. Farms here and there. Cows. Sheep. There's an old stone fence. When I went to visit when I was a young girl, the farmer who lived there said that was the favorite spot for my grandfather to sit. He was quite amused that I'd automatically gone to the fence and sat down to look at the ocean. They were very nice to me. Even though it was haying time and they needed to use every moment cutting and raking the hay, they stopped and fed me coffee and cake."

When her gran said sheep, Frances instinctively reached into her pocket to feel the bit of wool she had gathered. When she did, she turned her head sharply to the right. There was nothing there except the bulrushes and the water, but she could have sworn she'd seen someone.

"Ghosts!" she said. She meant the momentary image that had made her turn to look, but her gran thought she'd meant something else.

"Yes. Those, too. The air was thick with them. People born under the glacier are supposed to be psychic. They can see things others can't. Sometimes they can see the future, sometimes the past."

"Superstition?"

"Yes, that's what it is. Superstition. Silly sort of thing."

"Ouiji boards and seances?"

"Sometimes, I guess. There was a lot of interest in that."

"Flimflammery," Frances said, but as she said it, she didn't feel good. She felt like she was betraying someone, someone who was trying to get her attention. She felt disappointment. She just about said she was sorry.

She stopped and looked around. It was a normal, bright sunny day in Manitoba. A muskrat was swimming in the canal. She kicked a rock and sent it splashing into the water.

The marsh was a sea of blue with islands of green bulrushes. There were red-winged blackbirds in the willows and on the bulrush stems. Three pelicans were gliding overhead, getting ready to land. They'd stopped coming for awhile but now they returned every year. At first there were only two. Now there were twelve. The year before, her class had made nests for wood ducks. These were dotted around the marsh. Two terns were fishing close to the shore.

"I love it here," she said. "I don't ever want it to change. This is the way it's supposed to be. People and animals living in harmony together. It's paradise."

3

Later, when Frances was alone in her room, she looked at the books. Some were poetry. That was easy to figure out from the lines. One was a translation of *The Robe*. She knew that because it said so in English at the front. Some of the books had been published in Iceland, some in Denmark, some in Manitoba.

One, though, hadn't been published anywhere.

It wasn't a whole book. The cover had been beautiful at one time. It was all swirls of green and red. Most of the pages had been cut out. Just the rough edges remained.

The pages that were left were handwritten. The writing was beautiful, with curving lines—not like the chicken scratches Frances made with her ballpoint. She ran her index finger along some of the letters, tracing their fluid movement.

I wish I could read these words, she thought, but she didn't recognize any of them. The words for pancakes and rolled sheep flank weren't used that often, she guessed.

That night she was restless. She kept dreaming and waking up but when she woke, she couldn't remember what she'd been dreaming. Her mother heard her and brought her a glass of milk.

"Too much sun," she said.

The next morning, Frances showed the handwritten book to her gran. It was a mess. Mold and water had obscured some of the words. Pages were stuck together. She put on the kettle and held the pages in the steam. She had to stop because the ink immediately began to blur.

Her mother was using the car, so Frances and her grandmother rode their bicycles into town. Over the causeway and down the pioneer road.

Frances always felt good riding on the pioneer road. There were only short sections of it left. Some parts had been grown over by poplar trees and hazelnut bushes. Other parts had been washed away as the lake eroded the shoreline. Still other parts had been plowed under. This piece was dirt with a yearly sprinkling of gravel. There were cottages and fishermen's houses on both sides. Many of them were surrounded by bush.

Tranquil was what came to mind. The paved highway was just to the west and cars zipped by constantly, but here there were toys in the yards and the shallow ditches. A husky was pulling a boy in a red wagon along the side of the road. In the spring, if there was high water, the ditches had fish in them. That spring she'd chased the fish by hand, slipping and sliding and falling in the water until she'd caught a good-sized jackfish with its hard, narrow snout. She'd carried it home in triumph. Her gran had praised her to the skies and baked the fish with stuffing. Emily had made her take a bath and lectured her on ladylike behavior.

By the time they reached the library, their shirts were soaked with sweat. They both sighed when they got into the air-conditioned interior, and Frances held up her arms to cool off. Gran took an Icelandic dictionary from the shelf, then settled at a table. Frances put out a notepad and a couple of pens.

After half an hour, Gran said, "It's hopeless. All I can make out on this page is Selkirk. I think it says we arrived in Selkirk. On the train. They're waiting for a boat to take them to Eddyville. They're staying with someone called Hjalmur Vigfusson. At least that's what I think it says. If I didn't have the English names, I wouldn't have figured that out. My Icelandic is too rusty and the words are too faded. Spray it with Lysol to make your mother happy and put it away on the shelf as a keepsake. Now, I'm going to have coffee with the girls. Do you want to come?"

Frances shook her head. She couldn't see herself spending the next hour crammed in a booth between four hot and sweaty women, sipping diet drinks while they rattled on about people she had never met.

She felt terribly discouraged. She stood outside the library weighing the book in her hand. She could just throw it away. Then it would be like she'd never found it. No one would ever know. Books got thrown away all the time.

She hesitated, taking a step toward the garbage can, then stepping back.

Why is this so hard, she thought. It's just a beat-up old book.

There were cars driving by, people in bathing suits walking to the beach. There was the rise and fall of the voices of the people lying on the sand and playing in the water. She was dappled by the shadows thrown by an old maple tree.

Everything was perfectly, absolutely normal right down to the two kids with their parents coming out of the tourist information building with plastic Viking helmets on their heads. Except that she felt as if she were in the midst of a terrible argument. It was like there was a crowd pushing and pulling her back and forth while they yelled and scolded.

Turmoil, she thought. That's what this is. Abruptly, she shoved the book into her saddlebag. Immediately, the turmoil subsided.

Sherlock Holmes, she said to herself, doesn't give up just because no one will provide him with information. But where to look? Who would care enough to help? None of the kids. They were into clothes and CDs. None of her mother's friends. They were into soap operas and cooking shows.

She went to the end of the street and sat on the breakwater. Normally she went to the dock. There was always something going on there. Kids fishing and swimming or paddling around on a skiff. The tourists always walked to the end to have their picture taken beside the lighthouse. The finger docks were packed with sailboats.

Where she was sitting on the breakwater, there was no one. There had been sand beach here at one time but when the dock was built, it changed the way the water flowed. Now the water came right up to the wall, and the beach was gone. Dark, rotting pilings from an old breakwater formed a jagged line. From here she could look across the south half of the bay back to her cottage. It was a flash of red roof among the poplars.

I'm so restless, Frances thought. She was sitting with her legs over the breakwater, throwing stones and twigs into the water. My feet are restless. My head is restless. The water shone like polished aluminum. The rock was so hot that she kept lifting her hands off it.

She shielded her eyes with one hand. She pushed herself to her feet. Her back was to the water and she was looking across the street at an old woman sitting on the porch of the old folks' home.

Frances had always been afraid of the OFH. Wrinkle Land, the kids called it. They believed that anyone who went in the front door came out old, zapped by an energy beam that sucked them dry, just like the apples zapped by Gran's dehydrator.

Wrinkle Land, she thought, staring at the front porch. A couple of her cousins volunteered there, reading to people whose eyesight had failed. They'd disproved the energy-beam theory by returning unwrinkled. Because Frances liked to read, they'd asked her to volunteer, too, but she'd said no. There was something about the porch and the pillars and the old people with their canes and walkers that scared her. When she passed, she usually looked the other way. Sometimes there was a hearse parked at the back, and when she saw that, she made a detour.

"We all get old," her gran had said. "Look at me." Except her gran did sit-ups in the middle of the living room and danced the polka. The only time she needed a cane was when she broke her leg skiing.

Frances stood there chewing on her upper lip the way she did whenever she was trying to make up her mind about something. She glanced at her watch. Gran and her friends were good for another hour.

She raced back to the cottage, skidding around corners, bouncing over the washboard on the island road. She stuffed her saddlebags with books, then raced back to town. She leaned her bike against a maple tree that was in front of the OFH. She stacked the books into a pile, then wrapped her arms around them.

The same woman in a wheelchair was sitting on the porch. In spite of the heat she had a tartan blanket wrapped around her legs.

"Do you read Icelandic?" Frances asked.

The woman stared at her, then looked away, her lips pursed as if she were trying to remember if she did or not. Finally she looked back, then raised one arm and pointed inside. The high wooden doors were propped open.

Looking from sunlight into darkness, Frances couldn't see anything. She took a deep breath and plunged through the door into the shadows. She stopped and waited for her eyes to adjust. Gradually she made out a large foyer with overstuffed chairs, potted ferns on high stands, and a fireplace with a large mirror over it. She stepped forward gingerly the way she did when testing new ice to see if it would hold her weight.

On the other side of the foyer a woman in a white uniform was sitting at the desk. Frances tiptoed over to her.

"I've brought some Icelandic books," Frances whispered.

The woman with the white cap stared at her for a few moments, then pointed down the hall.

They're all mute, Frances thought. A whole old folks' home of mutes. All they could do was point. Maybe they'd taken a vow of silence.

She backed down the hall, keeping her eyes on Whitey. Where, she wondered, was she supposed to go? The hall seemed endless. Doors opened on both sides.

Finally she saw a small projecting sign that said LIBRARY.

"Hello," she whispered. "Anybody here?" She leaned in and peered around the pile of books. The library seemed empty, but suddenly a man in a wheelchair darted from behind a bookshelf. He was wearing a wine-colored cardigan and dark pants. He had on bedroom slippers. His glasses were perched on his head. He sat there glaring at her.

"Books," Frances said. She felt her voice go up an

octave. She hated that. Whenever she was nervous, her voice went Mickey Mouse.

The man in the wheelchair pointed at a desk. Another mute, she thought. She dumped the books on the desk. "My mother said to donate them." The diary was on top. She snatched it off.

He thrust out his hand. Without thinking, Frances shoved the diary at him. He opened it and looked at the inside back cover. *"This is my book. Ingibjorg."* He snapped the cover shut. "Do you want to donate it to the library?"

"You can talk!" Frances said, then clapped her hand over her mouth.

He was looking at the pile of books. He turned his head to stare at Frances.

She didn't try to explain. Every time she did, it just made things worse. She took a deep breath and let it out. Breathing with her stomach always helped her to calm down.

"No." She put out her hand for the diary. "Just these others." She took a deep breath. "I need help translating this into English." If her mother could go out every day and talk to strangers, she could, too.

The man paused and studied her, looking her up and down. She wished that she'd got dressed up, that she wasn't in her ragged shorts and a T-shirt that said

CHAOS RULES. She knew that she was covered in dust but hoped it wasn't obvious.

I'm not as frivolous as I look, she thought, remembering her mother saying people judged you in the first thirty seconds.

"Help means that you will do the work and from time to time you will need assistance. You can read Icelandic, then, and don't know the occasional word?"

Frances shook her head.

"What you meant to say was you want someone to do the work for you while you fritter away the summer at the beach."

Frances nodded, then shook her head. She was trying to decide whether to name him Glittery Eyes or the Old Grouch. She settled on the Old Grouch.

"Yes, I want someone to translate it for me. No, I don't fritter. At least, I don't think I do. Not more than anybody else, anyway." He handed her back the book and started to turn his wheelchair away.

"Wait," Frances said, feeling desperate. "I had a great-great-amma named Ingibjorg." The man stopped. "Maybe it's hers. I don't know. I can't help it if I can't read Icelandic. My great-greats came here in 1888."

"That so?" he said, turning around slowly. "Who were these great-greats, if I may ask?"

"Sigtrigur Jonsson and his daughter, Ingibjorg Sigtrigursdottir. Ingibjorg was my great-great. There also was Sigtrigur's sister, Hjotun. She didn't stay." Desperately, Frances dredged up anything she could remember hearing her relatives say. "They had a farm southwest of town. It was called Midas because there was a natural meadow there. My gran and I put up a sign with the name on it. Right at the gate. My great-great-afi was very ill after they came here."

"Well, then, if your gran knows enough to put up a place name, she should be able to translate this for you."

"She tried," Frances said. She wished she'd read her mother's books on how to negotiate. "She says it's been too long a time."

"Throw it in the garbage," he said. "That's where most of the old books have gone. People die and their children and grandchildren take everything out to the dump."

"I can't help what other people do," Frances said. She could feel her temper starting to rise. "I'm not other people."

The Old Grouch held out his hand. Once again she gave him the book. This time he looked at it more carefully. He pried open a page.

"I found it in an old trunk in the barn."

"It's only part of a book. Most of the pages are

missing. Hard to read with the mold and the mice and the water."

That wasn't a yes, but it wasn't a no, either. "I've tried to get the pages apart," she offered. "I'm afraid of wrecking them."

"My hands aren't so steady," he replied. She noticed the book was trembling. "Slip your finger under the frontispiece. Be gentle."

Frances wriggled her index finger into the opening at the top. She twisted her finger to the right, then to the left. She could feel the paper pop loose. She curled her finger and pulled up. Little by little, the paper separated.

Once she had one corner done, she pried loose the other three. As she worked, the dry mustiness of the book made her want to sneeze. Even the inside of the cover had been written on.

"Come to the light," he said. He wheeled himself to a window. She followed, then held the book up so he could see it.

"July 1, 1888." He held his shaking finger to indicate the first piece of writing. Below, water had smudged the carefully penned lines. Frances waited.

"Take it home," he ordered, and her heart sank. "See if you can separate the first two pages. No more."

"You'll help?" Frances asked.

"If I'm alive, I'll look at them. Bring a notebook and two pencils. An eraser. No pens. There'll be revisions."

"I'm Frances," she said, finally introducing herself.

He didn't introduce himself. Instead he sat there studying her like she might have studied an insect she had caught in the marsh.

Suddenly he nodded and turned around to look at the books she had brought. Frances crept out of the room, sighed with relief, then raced down the hallway. She slowed to a walk at the front desk, smiled quickly at Whitey and scooted across the foyer. A lot of old people were now sitting in the chairs. She bounded down the steps.

He'll help, she thought. If he's alive tomorrow, he'll help.

4

Frances went to the café to collect her gran. The girls were just paying for their soft drinks. A couple of them gave her a quick hug. When she was small, she'd always sat scrunched in a booth with them. During the summer they bowled together and during the winter they curled. She had got used to watching them knock down pins and play close ends. Now that she was older, if one of them wasn't able to make it, she filled in.

When she and Gran were riding their bikes, Frances said, "You know, I've been thinking. This could be my great-great's diary or something like that. What do you think?"

Her gran didn't take the bait. When they stopped to buy milk, all she wanted to talk about was how Frances was going to have to spend some time studying math if she was going to improve her grades next year. Any time her gran didn't want to talk about something, she brought up mathematics.

Frances didn't want to hear it. The summer was for swimming and fishing and canoeing and picking berries and lying around reading novels and getting a sun tan and maybe, maybe even meeting boys, if any ever turned up at the island. The best place to meet boys was at the dock, but to do that she had to get into town on her own and hang around soaking up the rays. The trouble was that everyone knew her and knew her gran and her mother and they were always saying, "Oh, I saw Frances in town. She was enjoying being on the dock." Then her mother would have a fit. "No gallivanting," her gran would say. "Or it's off to a nunnery with you." That was the trouble with a gran who'd read *Hamlet*.

Trounced, Frances thought. Trounced with words.

"Don't always be using such big words," her mother said once. "It makes you sound affected."

"If you didn't want her to use big words," her gran had replied, "you shouldn't have taught her to do crossword puzzles when she was in grade one." They were always going on like that. Sometimes it made her feel like she was being pulled apart. Whoops, there goes an arm, there goes a leg. Just lost a kidney.

When they were back at the cottage, her gran lay in the hammock. Her mother went out and sat in a deck chair beside her. Frances could hear them quietly talking. When they kept their voices down like that it was usually because they were talking about her. Their words became rigid and stiff, with little hooks like Old English script. It wasn't a humdinger argument like when they'd battled it out over whether to spank or not to spank. Her gran had won for the non-spanking side even though Frances had drawn all over the living-room wall with lipstick.

Gran came in and made a salad and hot dogs and lemonade but instead of hanging around to chat, she disappeared into her bedroom. Later, after Frances's mother had gone off to sell a cottage to two yuppies with a puppy, her gran came back out.

"Tell me about the great-greats," Frances said.

"Sleeping dogs," Gran answered. When she was nervous she put her fingers on the table like she was going to play the piano, then moved her thumbs up and down against each other.

"It's history," Frances said. "I mean, what kind of skeletons can we have in our closet?"

"Skeletons can dance."

Frances seldom saw her gran looking like this. She didn't look sad or angry, just like she was looking somewhere far away at something Frances couldn't see.

"You said you'd ask her if I can go to Iceland with you on the charter."

"I mentioned it. She still doesn't think it would be a good idea."

Frances sighed and shook her head. She'd asked her mother if she could go with her gran but Emily said they couldn't possibly afford it. For the next few weeks there was no mention of the charter. Finally, Frances had asked her gran to try again.

"I think I'll go for a ride," Frances said. She was disappointed. Not devastated, not destroyed. Once her mother made up her mind about something she hardly ever changed it.

Frances had thought to go to town but when she got to the highway, she turned south. She often went riding along the country roads. She'd pick strawberries or saskatoons. Sometimes she'd bring some back to the cottage.

She went south, then west. It was only when she realized which road she was on that she knew she was going to the old farm. No one had ever said she shouldn't go there by herself. She'd just never gone alone before.

She got off her bike, trying to make up her mind if she should go back or go forward. Finally, she got back on her bike and started forward. She could see the gray barn roof that was starting to sag in the middle.

When she was little, the barn had seemed really

big, but now that she was older, it didn't seem so large. It was set well back from the road, then just north of that the clapboard house and behind that the remnants of the original log cabin. The house was very small. There had only been four rooms. Still, it must have seemed like a palace because the log cabin had just been one room divided by hanging blankets.

She got off her bike before she reached the gate. The road was crushed limestone. Her feet and the bike's tires raised clouds of white dust. She squinted her eyes. The yard was overgrown with thistles and hay. An old hay rake was rusting in one corner. Some machine she didn't know the name of had collapsed beside it. The machine was all askew.

Askew made her feel better. It felt like an old friend.

She wished a bird would sing or a car go by, its tires whirring on the crushed rock.

Surrounding the house and yard was a line of birch trees. They were so old that many had died. The trunks of those that remained were thick, and the white bark was covered with black scars.

She pushed open the gate, then carefully closed it. A local farmer kept some sheep on the property. The area around the house was fenced, but the fence posts were rotten and, from time to time, the sheep managed to get through the wire. At one time the house had been painted white with yellow trim. Now the paint had been scrubbed off by the wind. Beyond the fences there were fields of flax and canola. The flax was a sea of pale blue. From a distance it looked like water. The canola was acres of bright yellow. The scent of the flowers was heavy and sweet.

Frances stood at the gate, uncertain. She wanted to go to the remains of the log cabin. Four walls hardly higher than her head. The bark had fallen off and the moss and mud that had been used to chink the cracks had dried and fallen out. There was a door frame and a door made of planks. There were window frames on each side of the door but there were no windows in them. She wanted to put her hands on the walls that were still standing.

She stood there, staring at the cabin, trying to imagine her great-great-amma and afi, Ingibjorg and Gunnar, eating meals in it, sleeping in it. There had been no roads. The bush was thick and tangled. Before Gunnar dug drainage ditches, there had been pools of water where the mosquitoes bred. She'd heard from her gran how large piles of green branches were burned to create smudges that would keep away the mosquitoes. You stood in the smoke and choked or outside the smoke and were eaten alive.

There were things that she had been told that she remembered. Not whole stories, but bits and pieces of things. The trouble was that every time her gran would start to tell her something, her mother would say, "What do you want to be talking about that for? You spend all your time talking about the past, you won't have any time to plan the future." Emily believed that the secret of success was to carefully plan the future. No wasting time on things that didn't take you anywhere.

Frances left her bike beside the gate and followed the path they'd cut on the day when they'd found the trunk. The grass was hip high. In years when the hay crop was poor, the farmer cut the grass with a hay mower. In good crop years like this he didn't bother. In a few weeks, he'd run some sheep in and let them eat the yard clear. She liked the sheep. When she'd been little, the farmer had let her ride them.

The path curved around the east side of the house and led to a semi-circle of mountain ash with their dusty green leaves and clumps of orange berries that would turn bright red in the fall. This was where Ingibjorg's father was buried. Frances had heard many times how Gunnar had dug the mountain ash out of the bush and brought them to the farm. Ingibjorg had planted them. There was a small head-stone that lay flat with the ground. Her gran came here every year to cut the grass and weeds. She always planted some flowers on the grave.

Some grass had collected on the gravestone. Frances brushed it off. Sigtrigur Jonsson. That meant his father was named Jon. When they emigrated to Canada, they gave up the Icelandic tradition of naming the children after the father's first name. If they'd kept it up, Frances wouldn't be a Sigurdsson. She'd be Egillsdottir because her father's first name had been Egill. If she'd had a brother, he'd have been Egillsson. It seemed simple enough. If your dad was Robert, then you were Robertsdottir, or Robertsson.

She wished her father had a grave. If she couldn't have a father, at least she could have done like Gran. She could have gone out once a year and cleaned it up. Now and again, when she was lonely, she could have taken flowers and just sat there. Some kids were scared of graves, but she wasn't. She'd been coming out here since before she could remember. She'd helped weed and plant flowers. She and her gran had sat in the shade of the mountain ash to eat their lunch. She'd caught bees here in a jar with a lid full of punched holes. She'd taken them home and fed them sugar water before letting them go.

The thought flitted through her mind that she should bicycle out to the cemetery to visit her great-greats. She'd never gone to visit them.

A croaking sound startled her. She looked up. She had to shield her eyes against the sun and, at first, she could not tell what sort of bird was sitting on the barn roof. It was large and white with a few dark markings. She thought it might be a magpie.

She moved to the side to get a better look. The bird called again and this time its croaking sounded like someone chopping wood with a dull ax. Only a raven made that sound.

It walked a few steps on the barn ridge. A white raven, Frances thought. Some of the fishermen said they had seen a white raven but they were so rare that most people thought the fishermen were spinning tales. Some of her friends were afraid of ravens but she knew that the Nordic god Odin carried two ravens, Huginn and Muninn, on his shoulders. Early every morning they flew all over the world and when they returned, they whispered their news into Odin's ears so that he knew everything that was going on.

Huginn, she thought. Where is Muninn?

As if in answer to her question, a black raven hopped up beside the white raven. A purple sheen glowed from its head and shoulders.

Frances admired ravens for their intelligence and their sense of humor. She'd seen them tease her gran, watching her plant flowers, then flying down and pulling out a plant and dropping it on the ground. Her gran had chased the raven away, then put the plant back. The raven had returned and pulled it out.

He's laughing, her gran had said the fifth time she put the plant back. He thinks it's a great joke.

All at once, Frances shivered. A cloud had passed in front of the sun. The whole yard was in shadow. Her upper arms and back were cold, as if an October wind had sprung up. The ravens watched her intently. She found it hard to quit staring at the white raven.

Slowly she backed away, ran down the path and climbed onto her bike. The cloud passed and the sun was as bright as ever.

Her head felt like it was on fire. Time to go home and get a drink of water, she thought. When she looked back, the barn roof was rippling with heat waves. The ravens had disappeared.

"Have a nice time in town?" her gran called.

"Oh, yeah, fine," Frances answered. She felt strange as she gulped down three glasses of water, one after the other. She hardly ever lied to her gran. They always shared their secrets, but it was like something was pulling her and something else was pushing her and she couldn't make it out or explain it.

5

....
....

The next day she went back to the OFH with her saddlebags filled with more books. The Old Grouch was waiting for her on the front porch. He didn't say hello, Frances, or how are you, Frances, or have you got the book with you, Frances. Instead, he said, "Have you got two dollars?"

Frances checked in her pocket. She nodded.

"Good. Take the books inside. Then I want you to push me to the ice-cream parlor and buy me a chocolate cone and not one of those for seniors. A real, full-size one." Frances stared at him. "You asked me to do some work for you. My fee is a chocolate cone."

"All right," Frances said, but she was thinking ice-cream extortion.

When he had the cone, they sat at one of the plastic sidewalk tables.

"Show me the book," he demanded. "Put it down

flat on the table. I won't get ice cream on it. Aren't you going to have a cone?"

"I don't have any more money," Frances replied.

"Kids nowadays eat too much junk food anyway. When you get to be my age, it doesn't make any difference. Get out your pencils and paper." He waited until Frances was ready, then he bent forward.

"How old was your great-great-amma when she came to Canada?" he suddenly asked.

Frances felt flustered by the unexpected question. "I don't know." She paused. "Wait a minute." She remembered what her gran had said about the trunk. "She was thirteen. The same age I am now."

TOG nodded. "Write this down," he said.

"Boarded our ship at 5:30 this morning. Two large rooms filled with beds," he dictated. "No, that's not right. It says beds piled on top of each other. It has to be bunks. It's a description of the cabin of a ship. I can't get it word for word but it says, *There's cold water all the time and hot water three times a day. There are bathrooms for men and women. The ship is leaving and the weather is good.*

"July 04/88. I'm seasick. Some people are singing hymns. I feel like I want to die. My father brought me some milk to drink but I couldn't drink it. My aunt is ill also and says she wishes she'd never left Iceland.

"They have divided the hold in half and built a wall

between. On the other side from us are hundreds of Icelandic horses being taken to England. One of the men told me they are going to be used as pit ponies in the English mines. They will be lowered into the bottom of the mines and spend their whole lives in the darkness. I think that is terrible.

"It smells like we are living in a barn and when the ship rolls, everything from the horses comes into our living quarters. My father and some of the men are trying to block the bottom of the dividing wall. I can hear the horses crying. How frightening it must be. They were running free over the mountains in Iceland only a few weeks ago and now they're locked up in the hold. Maybe it is better that they don't know what the future is going to bring.

"July 05/88. I was feeling better today. One of the women brought me some bread and warm milk with sugar. I ate some of it. Most of the time, I've just been drinking cold water. Most people are getting used to the motion of the ship and are feeling better. The women who aren't seasick are knitting. One of the men brought a violin and he plays music now and again. I went up on deck today for the first time. That is when something strange happened."

He wasn't able to tell it to her all at once. He had to piece together sentences. Some words he had to guess at. Others were unreadable. Frances would write down a word, then another word, then he'd tell her to change them around. They worked for over an hour.

"That's enough for today," he said. "Push me back now. I get tired easily and then the angina starts."

On the way back, she casually said to him, "Do you know anything about ravens?"

He glanced back at her. "Why do you ask?"

"No reason," she said. One of the wheels on his wheelchair squeaked. She'd have to remember to bring some oil for it.

It was another hot, dry day. Tourists jammed the sidewalk in front of the burger take-out. She kept saying excuse me and edging forward. A large woman in lime-green shorts and orange top and a purple hat was blocking their way. Frances raised her voice.

"Excuse me, may we get through?" Reluctantly, afraid she'd lose her place in line, the woman edged out of their way.

"You can speak up when you have to," TOG said. "Why aren't you as assertive about ravens?"

They had stopped at the corner. There was a Cadillac turning in front of them.

"I saw two," Frances said. "A black one and a white one. I didn't know if you'd believe me if I told you about the white one."

"Rare," he replied, "but not unknown. Sometimes

they're piebald. What do you want to know?"

"Anything, I guess. I know about Huginn and Muninn."

"Do you now? And where did you hear about them?"

Time seemed to slow down then. She'd felt this way before, as if she was moving in amber, sunlit water. The noise of the traffic and the sharp laughter and the chattering voices all faded away. First one car, then another refused to give way. They ended up waiting in the middle of the street. Then Frances found it hard to get the wheelchair over the curb. A knot of people came out of the store and stopped in a cluster around them while they discussed what to do next.

Frances took a deep breath and gripped the handles of the wheelchair. When this happened, it was as if she was fading into some other place—a place full of foreign sounds and smells.

Gradually the moment passed and she said, "I've been reading the sagas in English. My mother wouldn't like it. She doesn't like anything Icelandic. She's into the Royal Family. She wants to go to England and do the royal tour."

"Ravens," TOG said contemplatively. "Some people think if they visit your window, you will die soon. If a raven sits on a church steeple, a relative will die."

"What about on a barn roof?"

"Nothing that I know of but I can check. If you see a raven being aggressive or plunging down in flight, he is protecting you from evil spirits. It pays to treat them well."

"Ingibjorg," Frances said. "I'd like to learn lots about her. I like that name."

When she got back to the cottage, her mother was there.

"What are you doing, child?" she asked. "You look quite distracted."

"I think I'd better lie down," Frances replied. "Mad dogs and Englishmen. I shouldn't have gone riding in the noonday sun." She was still feeling the effects of the moment on the street. She felt confused.

"You could have worn a hat and your sunglasses," her gran said.

"I'll be fine. Maybe I'll have a cold shower first."

The thunder started before she was out of the shower. She heard it rumbling in the distance. By the time she was drying herself off, it was closer. The sky was still clear but the thunder was loud and sharp and lightning zigzagged down in bright, sudden bolts.

"Let's go watch it from the porch," her gran said.

Frances got her comforter and stretched it out on the porch overlooking the lake. Gran brought them two pillows each. In the east there was a black line of clouds with a high thunderhead moving across the lake toward them. A sudden wind picked up, making little pucky ripples on the water. It came in short, sharp gusts. In between the gusts the air was absolutely still.

As the clouds came closer, Frances could smell the rain. The thunder broke right overhead, jarring the cottage so hard that it shivered. A bolt of lightning tore down the sky into the water. Afterwards, the sharp smell of ozone pricked her nostrils.

Lightning bolts struck all along the lake. Sometimes there were three or four so close together that the thunder when it reached them came in waves.

"Throwing chairs," Frances said. When she was little, she'd been afraid of the thunder and her gran had told her that it was just the giants upstairs throwing the furniture around.

The lightning stopped. Then the rain came in gusts and, finally, in gusty sheets. Suddenly, it was a downpour. It pounded on the roof, overflowed the gutters. The wind picked up, forcing them to pull down the shutters, but Frances stayed on the porch, listening to the wind and the rain.

Sometimes emotions are like that, she thought. Powerful, raging, overwhelming, but they don't last. With that thought, she fell asleep.

When she woke up, the storm had passed. The sun was out again. She yawned and stretched. Her cat, Samantha, was curled up beside the door.

Frances wandered out the front door. The two steps were right on the sand. There was a line of birch trees. Beyond that was the beach. It had been some storm, she realized, for driftwood had been driven right up to the steps. The beach itself was washed flat by the waves.

She was wearing flip-flops and stubbed her toe. Her left flip-flop came off. She stooped to pick it up and noticed a piece of dark wood. She gave it a push but it stayed in place.

She scooped some of the sand away. The top of the wood was no bigger than her thumb but as she dug down, it widened into a board. The board was charred.

A piece of wood from a wiener roast, she thought, except that it was standing on end.

They often had wiener roasts in the evenings. She and Gran would scour the beach for some dry drift-wood and make a small bonfire. Then they'd cut some willow sticks, strip off the bark and roast wieners and then marshmallows. She was always dropping her wieners or marshmallows in the sand. She dusted them off and ate them anyway. You'll get worms, her mother said, but she hadn't, at least not yet.

The piece of wood wouldn't budge. It was down deep. More than a foot of sand had been washed away by the storm.

Frances took one of her old metal shovels from under the cottage. All her toys were there from when she was little. She dug around the board. It was more than a board, she realized. It was a beam and a good solid one at that. Two by six. It went down about six inches and then she hit something solid. She kept digging and gradually uncovered a crossbeam.

She knocked lightly on her gran's bedroom door. They both went back outside.

"The foundation of the old house," her gran said. "Burned down years ago. Before you were born. Before I was born. I didn't realize that it was still there. These things get buried and you forget about them. Trust you to dig it up. This was the old homestead."

"I thought the farm was the old homestead."

"What are you two up to?" her mom asked. She was standing on the porch beaming. That meant she'd sold a Cozy Cottage to a Lovely Couple. That meant they were going to go into town for Chinese food. Pan-fried shrimp, lemon chicken, sweet and sour ribs. Pots of green tea.

"The storm uncovered the foundation of the old house."

"Cover it up," her mother said. "There are rusty nails in it. I don't want anyone getting blood poisoning."

Reluctantly, Frances covered the foundation. On the ride into town, no one mentioned her find. Gran never said anything about the diary.

Her mother told them all about her latest sale. Good people, she said. Good people, Frances knew, were people who bought something from her. People who didn't buy from her weren't bad people; they just weren't smart enough to recognize an opportunity when it stared them in the face. When Frances had complained to her grandmother about her mother's attitude, her gran had said that it must be hard to be charming every day of your life to strangers. Frances thought about that. She had a hard enough time being charming to her friends, never mind strangers. After that, she cut her mother some slack.

Cover it up, she thought, as she lay in bed. The wind had started up again and a birch tree that grew beside her window kept rubbing against the glass. She'd just start to fall asleep and then she'd wake up, certain that someone was trying to get her attention.

Under the glacier, she thought unexpectedly, just as she fell down a long dark hole into sleep. She wondered for an instant what it was like under a glacier, and then it was morning.

Her mother's car was gone. This was her busy season. This was when she filled up the bank account against the doldrums of winter. Her gran's bike was gone. There was a note saying, "Eat something decent for breakfast. No CoCo Puffs." There weren't any CoCo Puffs. Once when Frances was about eight, she'd wanted nothing but CoCo Puffs for about a week. Since then it had become a family joke.

She got herself some fruit and cheese and a glass of orange juice. Just as she came into the living room, Samantha arched her back and her fur stood up. Frances just about tripped and dropped the plate. For a nano-second, she thought there was someone sitting on the couch. She hadn't been looking at the couch. It was off to one side, just at the edge of her vision. She turned to look but there was no one there.

She looked at Samantha, whose fur was beginning to settle. If anyone had seen the two of them, they'd have been sure they were both nuts. She could hear Jimmy Rogers saying, "Man, that Sigurdsson girl, she and her cat are crazy. I dropped by to say hi and there the two of them were, both of them looking like someone had handed them a hot wire, hair in the air, staring at this couch. Wonk. Wonk."

Frances swallowed and blew out her breath. A cold shiver ran over her body. She gave herself a shake and went out onto the porch to eat her breakfast, but every so often she snuck a look at the couch.

I'm sneaking looks at my own couch, she thought. She wondered what she expected to see.

She had, her mother constantly reminded her, an overactive imagination, just like her father. It was about the only time that her father was mentioned.

He'd been a painter and had gone off one evening in his canoe to paint the wilderness. They'd found the canoe upside down on the shore, his life jacket tied to his paint box instead of on him, and no sign of his body.

They never found him and it had left a question in their lives. Was he somewhere on the bottom of the lake, drifting with the current, or had he staged the whole thing and gone off to live the footloose life of an artist in Spain or Portugal? It would have been easier if they'd found his body. That way she would at least have known how to feel. How can you grieve for someone if you think they might not really be dead but off some place where the weather is good year round, drinking wine and going to parties?

She never knew whether to be sad or angry. If he were dead, then it would be normal to be sad. She didn't want to think about his bones moving restlessly around the bottom of the lake. If he were alive, then she was angry because he'd never once written, never once remembered a birthday or a Christmas. Not knowing how to feel about him made her feel frustrated and helpless.

She found a real shovel in the tool shed. To get it she had to fight thirteen hundred spiders and tear down webs as thick as dish towels. She dug up the footing. That, she'd learned from the conversation over supper, was what it was called. Because they were on a sandbar, just a couple of feet above the level of the lake, there couldn't be a basement so houses had been put on wooden footings. Square beams sawn by hand from the trunks of trees.

She had quite an excavation by the time her gran returned.

6

"Can't you leave well enough alone?" Gran asked. She was wearing a blouse, khaki shorts and running shoes. She was carrying her bike helmet. "You'd better cover that up before your mother gets home."

Frances glared at her.

"There was a big old house here," Gran said. "Painted yellow. It had lots of gingerbread on it and on top there was a widow's walk. The widow's walk had a fence made of black painted iron. You could see all the way to the other side of the lake from up there."

"You never told me! I thought you didn't like secrets. You've been keeping this a secret."

"That's all I'm saying until that's covered up. I don't want to have to listen to your mother go on all day and all night about how I'm doing a poor job of taking care of you while she's off working her heart out to keep a roof over our heads and food in our bellies."

Reluctantly, Frances replaced the sand. Along the footing and the cross footings she had found, she stuck bits of driftwood.

In my mind's eye, I'll be able to see the whole picture when I've got them all in place, she thought. And who knows what else I'll find.

When she went inside, her gran was making baking powder biscuits.

"What are you and Mom fighting about?"

"We're not fighting." She had that short, clipped voice she used when she was annoyed or upset. "Did you see us fighting?"

"You were whispering. When you guys whisper, it's so I won't hear. When you don't want me to hear, it's because you're disagreeing about something."

"Your mother should never have brought that box home. She should have left it where it belonged. All she thinks about is money, money, money." She was cutting out biscuits and each time she said money, she gave the cutter a twist. "You'd think we were a penny away from the poorhouse."

"The house that was here must have been pretty big."

"It was owned by a very rich man."

"You said our family was poor."

"Your great-great-great-grandfather was a farmer and a carpenter. They brought their clothes and his tools. They had a few English pounds from selling their sheep. You want to know anything more about this family, you ask your mother. She makes the decisions around here. I'm just your grandmother." She thumped down the pan. The pans took a beating when she was annoyed.

"I need the key to the shed," Frances said. "I want to pick up my blue blouse."

"Remember to pick up your math book," her gran replied.

They usually moved from their house in town to the cottage on April 1 and stayed there until the end of September. Emily rented out the house but they kept all their personal belongings in the shed.

The shed was long and narrow. It was where her gran and her afi had seamed on nets. They tied the nets to rollers at each end of the building, then walked their length tying the mesh to the side lines. Her gran had told her when they first started tying on nets for a fish company, they were paid one and a half cents a fathom. They walked endless miles over the months and years. The fine dust from the cotton nets settled in their lungs and made them cough in the mornings when they got up. It was terrible work. Before the fishing season they sometimes seamed on for twenty hours at a stretch and yet they never made enough to pay for their fuel and groceries. It was only when the air base was built on the edge of town and her afi had got a job as a janitor that they finally had a real income they could depend on.

Yet here was a large house owned by a rich man and it had been the family's at one time.

The thoughts rattled and banged around in Frances's head. It made no sense, and she hated things that made no sense.

They were always going back and forth getting things or dropping them off. Her mother was very organized and all the shelves and boxes were labeled. Frances found what she wanted in a box marked PHOTO ALBUMS.

She rummaged through the photo albums and found pictures of herself, her mother and her grand-parents. There were no pictures of her great-amma or her great-greats. She thought there might have been some of those old types of photos she'd seen at the museum—faded brown, stained with age—of people in rigid poses. She thought there might be a photo of her father. Most people had wedding photos taken. Lots of people took pictures when they were court-ing.

She looked for an obituary. There was nothing.

She knew that when some of her girlfriends broke up with their boyfriends, they cut the boys out of all their photos. Others just cut up the photos. She thought that she would not do that with her ex-boyfriends, when she finally had some, because it would be much more interesting to have the evidence. Her own rogues' gallery. She wondered if her mother had cut up any pictures of her father.

As she sorted through the pictures, she found duplicates of her gran, Emily and herself. She decided to take them so that she could paste them on a genealogical table. When she was finished, she would have a record of her ancestors all the way back to the Vikings. She'd know exactly who she was and where she came from.

When she got back to the cottage, her gran was deep into an article on some movie star breaking up with her husband.

"You said you'd talk if I covered up the foundation," Frances said.

Her gran looked over the top of the magazine at her. Frances could see that she was thinking about what to tell her. She got that same look when they played cribbage and they were trying to out-psych each other.

"There are all these old stories. Gossip and silliness as your mother says. There's no need to resurrect them. Your langa langamma was…different. There were always stories about her. You know what that's like."

"I'm different," Frances said. "Instead of blonde hair, I've got black. I go out in the sun and I turn instant brown. Everybody else is blonde."

"You're a throwback, I guess. There were Spanish ships wrecked on the coast of Iceland. Some people say there were even Moors. In those days if you made it to shore, you didn't get on a plane and fly home. You stayed. Most people from that area are dark as ravens. It's not such a big deal. The rest of you looks like everyone else."

The moment her gran said that, Frances felt as though she'd heard the swish of wings and saw, once again, Huginn and Muninn on the barn roof. She wished she hadn't run away. She wished she'd been brave enough to listen to them whisper secrets in her ears.

Even as she thought it, she wasn't really sure she wanted to know. Wanting to know and knowing were two different things.

"What color was Ingibjorg's hair?" Frances asked.

"Black. So black that in the sun it shone purple. Gunnar was as blond as she was dark."

"There were ravens on the barn roof yesterday," Frances said, then stopped. She hadn't meant to mention that she'd been at the farm.

"Does your mother know you were there?" her grandmother asked.

Frances shook her head. She could see her gran weighing her thoughts, deciding what to tell her. She put down her magazine.

"They led a hard life. They were very poor. Lots of people left the settlement. They stayed."

"You're leaving something out. I can always tell when you're leaving something out. It's like when I asked about that Sally person and you told me she was a good housekeeper and made the best ginger snaps to have with tea. You didn't tell me that she'd also been to prison for robbing a bank."

"I thought the ginger snaps were more important. They were good ginger snaps. Since she's moved, I miss them." Frances stood there, her arms crossed in front of her. "One of the things people talked about was the raven assembly. Ingibjorg was…"

Then they heard Emily's car drive up and the door open and shut. Her grandmother picked up her magazine and started reading.

7

Frances tried to settle by reading a book. Reading nearly always took her mind off things, but today she could not concentrate.

A raven assembly. She thought she knew everything there was to know about her grandmother, but now she felt she didn't know her at all.

Frances dug into her money jar and took out two dollars. She first went to the library. She took every book that mentioned ravens and piled them onto the reading table. Then she started skimming through them.

There were all sorts of facts. They nest in single pairs. They mate for life. They lay four to seven eggs that are greenish with brown. Their beaks and feet are black. There were native stories and English stories and European stories about ravens, but none of them mentioned a raven assembly.

He was waiting for her in the foyer. He'd put on a

sports jacket and tie. His unruly white hair was brushed back. He had the diary sitting in his lap. Behind him, the ferns dripped like green waterfalls.

He held out his right hand. As she shook it, he said, "My name is Eric Johannson. I didn't introduce myself before because I doubted you'd remain interested. Most young people have a short attention span."

She was dressed in her best shorts and top. Icelanders, even those who had been in Canada for five generations, put a lot of importance on how you dressed, her gran had told her more than once. That's why when they went to a wedding or tombola, they starched and ironed until their clothes were perfectly pressed.

"You're not all dusty today," he observed.

"I didn't race here. Besides, the town truck watered the road."

"Well," he said, "there are thirty-five flavors and I'm going to try as many of them as possible, so we might as well get going."

He didn't want to sit at the table in front of the ice-cream parlor so she pushed him to the sidewalk that ran along the beach. There were a lot of people splashing about in the water. A group was playing volleyball. Some families had spread blankets under the row of maple trees that sat on a grassy verge between the beach and the back lane.

"I used to walk along here every day, summer and winter," he said. "See that house?" He pointed to a two-story white frame house. It was like a wooden box. "That was my home. I dug the basement by hand. It took me all one winter. People thought I was crazy tackling that job with a shovel, but persistence and patience pay off."

Frances would have believed him if he'd said he'd dug the basement with a spoon. He had that determined set to his chin.

She wheeled him to the end of the sidewalk and would have pushed him farther to where there was shade and hardly any people, but he waved his hand for her to stop.

"I like to be where things are happening," he said. "I get more than enough quiet at the old folks' home."

They stopped beside a concrete take-out stand that was right on the beach. A steady stream of holidayers came up to the booth for food and drinks. There were brightly colored umbrellas and blankets everywhere. A group of children were kicking a plastic ball back and forth. Voices rose and fell around them.

"Something strange happened," Frances said, prompting him. "That was the last thing you read. She said she went up on deck and something strange happened."

"There was a thick fog," he answered. Because of the heat, some of the ice cream had dripped on his fingers. She went to the take-out stand, got a napkin and wet it at the tap where people washed their feet before putting on their shoes. She gave it to him. He carefully wiped his fingers, then held up his notes to avoid the glare.

"She says it was so thick she could barely see across the deck. She says she was already in love with Gunnar and had decided she would marry him one day."

"That was the strange thing? That she met him?"

"No." Mr. Johannson sighed. Frances knew that sigh. It was the Sigh of Life. Older people used it to express how unbelievably ignorant the younger generation was. Her gran used it from time to time.

I said to Gunnar that I thought there were stowaways hiding on board. I thought I'd seen one in the lifeboat. He went and looked in it but didn't find anyone. When he came back, we talked about Canada.

"'They say there's all the food you can eat in Canada. No one has to eat grass to live,' I told him.

"'There's no sea or mountains or home fields where we're going,' Gunnar replied. He didn't want to leave Iceland but his relatives paid his passage rather than have to support him. His parents are dead.

"'What would you do if you stayed in Iceland?' I

asked him. 'The cattle are dead. The sheep are dead. You can't farm lava. I've listened to the men talking. They say there is work in Canada for anyone willing to work.'

"'And what good will that do me?'

"I didn't know what to say. An accident has made one leg slightly shorter than the other so that he has a limp. It makes it difficult for him to do farm chores. He was excluded from the rough and tumble games of the other boys. Instead, he spent his time reading and studying.

"Finally I said, 'We never know what some day might be a blessing.'" Mr. Johannson put down the notes.

"That's it?" Frances said. "They didn't get mushy like in *Titanic*?"

"This is real life." He looked at her disgustedly. "People didn't get 'mushy,' as you put it, at the drop of a hat."

"She married him."

"Later," he said. "When they were older. When he finished Normal School. Everyone knows that. He had a fine reputation as a teacher."

"Where are the big secrets?" Frances complained. "There has to be a big secret. Look at the way my mother is always trying to cover things up. I ask a question about the great-greats and it's all hush-

hush. What did they do? Run away together? I mean, she has fits. You know, today…" She was just going to say something about how she and the cat had their hair rise up but then let it slide.

"Today?"

"Nothing. I was just thinking. We've got this cottage built on top of what used to be a house. That's sort of like what the archeologists find." She was rambling. She knew she'd better shut up before she said more than she intended. "That's all?" she asked indignantly. "For a Rocky Road ice-cream cone?"

"If you can find someone to work cheaper, go ahead," he said. "I can't help it if the book is such a mess. It's slow going. At a dollar eighty for a cone, it works out to about twenty cents an hour."

She knew he was right. Still, she didn't have a very big pile of coins in her money jar. At one ice-cream cone a day the pile was going to diminish pretty rapidly. It wasn't like there was a lot of work coming her way. The take-out stands had done their hiring. The island cottages were mostly on sand so there wasn't much grass to cut. She could usually wheedle some money out of her mother, but that well ran dry pretty fast.

She pushed him back along the beach sidewalk. At his former house, he asked her to make a detour and go past the front so he could look at it.

"You know the tradition, do you?" he asked.

She shook her head. There was nothing special about the house. Like a lot of older houses in town, it was made of clapboard. It had high, narrow windows. Someone had put up lace curtains.

She doubted if there had been lace curtains when he lived there. There was an old-fashioned wire fence with a metal gate.

"When someone in town died, after they had the service, the funeral procession always went past the house so the deceased could have one last look at his home."

She looked sharply at him. He smiled and said, "Not that I'm expecting to kick the bucket just yet. I'm much too ornery to die."

When they had started again, Frances said, "What's a raven assembly?"

"You want to know the strangest things," he replied. She thought that, like her grandmother, he would avoid answering, but after he had thought for a bit, he said, "In Jon Arnason's folk tales the ravens hold a general assembly twice a year. In the spring they decide how to spend the summer. In the fall they pick a farm to stay at for the winter."

8

When Frances got back to the cottage, Gran was still reading magazines. She was addicted to stories about people being abducted by aliens. She took them as gospel. A couple of times she'd got Frances to go out at night with her on the road to town in hope that they'd be abducted by an alien space craft. She said it was the only chance she had of ever going into space. If she'd been younger, she would have become an astronaut.

Sometimes she'd go out in the evenings and when Frances asked where she was going, she'd say, "I have a date with the aliens," except Frances soon discovered that she was meeting her boyfriend. Occasionally he'd drive up to the cottage in his white BMW. He always brought flowers and a bottle of wine.

It embarrassed Frances to no end, thinking of her gran having a boyfriend. It was bad enough that she rode a bike in summer and a snowmobile in winter. She had even threatened to take up sky-diving.

Other people's grandmothers, Frances told her, spent their time in rocking chairs, knitting or baking cakes. The next time her gran was in town, she bought needles, wool and a cake mix. She gave them to Frances and said, "Go for it, kid."

Frances went and got her fishing rod.

"You want to help me scoop some minnows?" she asked Gran. The idea of a raven assembly had unnerved her. She didn't want to ask any more questions until her insides settled.

There was an offshore breeze, just enough to keep the mosquitoes away. The poplar leaves gently flashed pale green and silver.

They waded into the lake with the minnow net between them. They slipped and slid on the rocks, trying not to stub their toes. Five feet out the stones gave way to sand bottom. She could feel the rippled sand beneath her toes.

When they were out past their waists, they dipped the net down until the weighted edge was against the sand. The weight of the water bowed the net. Then they dragged the net toward the shore. When they reached the shallow water, they quickly lifted up the net. Inside it, a dozen silver minnows jumped.

Gently, Frances lifted them out and dropped them into a bucket of water.

"That raven assembly I was wondering about," she

said casually, as if anyone would know. "They hold them twice a year. Once in the spring. Once in the fall."

Her gran looked at her over her glasses. "You are a compendium of useless facts. That comes from starting crossword puzzles too early. You also probably know that if someone was good to them, they stayed at that person's farm. Grandma Ingibjorg always had ravens around. Some people said it was because she was svart. I think it was because she threw them scraps."

"Svart," Frances repeated. "You mean like black?"

"Just her hair."

"You know lots," Frances said, "and you're not telling me. It's like pulling teeth to learn anything about this family."

"I do not know lots, young lady. I know what I heard around the kitchen table. You've heard lots around the kitchen table. How much do you remember? It's just blah, blah, blah. In one ear and out the other. Repeat to me the details of the last five conversations your mother and I have had at supper time."

"Don't tell me. I don't care. The next time I go for the mail, I'll ask Moscow Mary."

Moscow Mary was eighty, wore three dresses at the same time, shoes that didn't match and stood at the front of the post office handing out flyers condemning the subjugation of the working class. She also smoked a short pipe.

"Don't you go tormenting her," Gran said.

"She loves answering questions. I'll ask her if my great-greats were running dogs of capitalism or whether they were oppressed workers. I'll bet she says they were rich exploiters of the poor and downtrodden."

"Your great-greats never trod on anyone. They took over an abandoned cabin and divided it into rooms with blankets. Ingibjorg planted beets and turnips and potatoes around the stumps. Her father, young lady, walked thirty miles to get a job working at a fish camp. When he came back he used his wages to buy a cook stove."

"That so?" Frances said.

"He cut the lumber for the floor by hand. You think…" Her gran stopped and glared at her. "You think you're smart, don't you? You're going to get me into trouble talking about stuff I'm not supposed to talk about. Well, it won't work."

"Tell me one thing about her. Something I don't know. She was your grandmother. She must have told you something."

"She was the same age as you are now when she packed up and came to Canada. She was so scared that she would die on the ship and be buried at sea that she made her father promise if she died, he wouldn't bury her until they got to land. I heard her telling my mother that while they played cribbage. I was about ten at the time and I thought it would be really romantic to be buried at sea. The trouble was I hadn't figured out that you don't get to enjoy your own funeral."

With that her gran clamped her lips shut. When she did that there was no point asking any more questions.

They rolled up the net. Then her grandmother went back to the cottage.

Frances caught one of the minnows, tapped its head against the bucket, then fixed it onto her pickerel rig. She put a minnow onto her second hook. She stretched her arm straight back, then swung it in an arc, releasing the line with her thumb at the top of the arc. The lead weight drew out the line. She watched the lead weight and pickerel-rig strike the water and disappear, then she took up the slack.

There was a forked stick set in the sand. She set the handle of the rod on the sand and leaned the rod on the fork, tested the tension of the line with her index finger, then lay on a blanket. She watched the small white clouds drifting across the lake. In the distance she could see the dark line of the dock and the masts of the sailboats.

The tip of the rod began to tremble. That was a nibble. She eased up onto one knee, felt the line with her finger. Gently, she picked up the rod. A fish was chewing on the minnow but it hadn't taken the hook.

She gave the line a slight pull—just enough to move it slightly away from the fish, just enough to tempt it to grab at its escaping prey. The line went tight and she instantly snapped the rod back, setting the hook.

She reeled in a small pickerel, pulled out the hook, threaded the pickerel onto her chain and put the fish back in the water so it'd stay fresh. She rebaited the hook.

When Wendy and Bryan showed up, she had two perch, a sunfish and the pickerel.

Wendy and Bryan came down from the city on weekends with their folks. Tenderfeet, Frances thought to herself, Greenhorns, the Uninitiated, Weekenders. But she was still glad to see them. They had their bikes and it meant she had company for cruising around town.

"You want to go into town?" Wendy asked. "For ice cream and things."

Frances knew what the things meant. Wendy had her eye on Jimmy Rogers.

Jimmy Rogers was a local dork. He was always standing in front of store windows or car mirrors and combing his hair. Some people became expert at riding skateboards, some people sailed. He was the master of hair-combing. He hair-combed in slow motion, with little pauses. What he really needed was a three-hundred-and-sixty-degree mirror in which to admire all of himself.

"Sure," Frances said. "Hi, Bryan."

Bryan glanced at her, smiled, then nodded before looking away.

Bryan was a year older than Wendy and that made him six months older than Frances. He had unruly red hair and freckles and was, in her mother's words, gormless—an English word her mother had picked up somewhere, sort of like she carefully bought expensive pieces of Prince Albert bone china. Frances had said to her mother that he was not gormless, he was just shy. Everyone couldn't be an outgoing real-estate agent.

She wasn't sure why she had defended him. Still, gormless was a word worth knowing. Bryan banged into tables and chairs and knocked over drinks and was always shuffling from one foot to the other in a kind of uneasy, loose-boned way. Why he wanted to tag along with his younger sister, she couldn't imagine.

"I've got to clean these fish first," she said. They followed her into the kitchen and while they watched, she cut off the heads and slit the bellies. She scraped out the insides, scaled the outside with the edge of the knife, then wrapped the fish and put it in the refrigerator.

"Gross," Wendy said. "I don't know how you can do that."

"Do you eat fish?"

"Yes, but we buy it at the shop."

"Somebody does it for you, then, that's all."

Wendy gave a shiver. When Wendy told her mother about the fish cleaning, it would give Mrs. Skillings something more to be disdainful about. Frances knew that Wendy's mom didn't quite approve of her. She'd heard that Mrs. Skillings had called her a little savage when she'd seen her foraging in the marsh. Frances took it as a compliment. She admired hunter-gatherers. It was her mother who had been offended. For the next two weeks she'd insisted that Frances wear nothing but dresses and skirts. Frances had been grateful that her mother was too busy having open houses to keep it up.

"You know," she said to Bryan. "You can eat the middle part of the cat tails. People pay big money for them in fancy restaurants. Here we've got all we want for free and nobody uses them. Except me." She had, too. Pulled them out, cut off the ends, peeled away the hard outer casing. She and Gran had steamed them. Marsh asparagus was what Gran called it.

They were having tea one day when Mrs. Skillings asked Frances what she'd been doing with herself.

"Catching frogs," she replied. "When I've got

enough we're going to have frog legs for supper." She loved the look on Mrs. Skillings' face. "These are frog leg sandwiches," she said, pointing to the open-faced sandwiches they'd been eating. The muscles in Mrs. Skillings' jaw tightened and her head tipped back slightly. She put down her tea cup. Because she was English, Emily was constantly trying to impress her.

Frances had been grounded for a week. "Frog leg pâté," her mother complained to her gran. "She must think we're barbarians." She'd turned to Frances. "And you had to tell her about Icelanders eating rotted shark and raw whale meat."

"Her husband is a dentist, for goodness' sake," Gran said. "When she's around, you carry on like a princess has arrived."

Frances had apologized to Mrs. Skillings. She ate so much crow that for the next two weeks, she was constantly spitting out feathers. It paid off, finally, because Wendy and Bryan were allowed to associate with her once more.

They decided to walk into town along the beach. The wind was to the north. The water was so low they could wade along the sandbars. The sand was hard packed. There was only one place where there was mud and that was where willows grew right to the water's edge. Behind was deep grass.

Wendy didn't like the feel of the mud between her

toes and was going to try to find a way behind the willows.

"Don't do it," Frances warned her. "There are wood ticks in the grass. Get one of those in your leg and we'll have to burn it out."

They wouldn't really have to burn it out. The best way to get them out was to pull them straight back with tweezers, but she wasn't going to tell Wendy that. The best way to keep her from being a wimp was to terrorize her a little. Besides, if Wendy did get ticks, Mrs. Skillings would be sure to blame Frances.

When they reached the town breakwater, they walked single file until they got to the dock area. They stopped to look at the gas boats the local fishermen used. Then they went to the ice-cream shop. Jimmy had a job scooping ice cream, but he wasn't working. They wandered down to the dock in case he was admiring his reflection in the water, but he wasn't there, either. Frances noted with satisfaction that although the sport fishermen were bringing in a few perch, they had no pickerel or sunfish.

She didn't feel like spending her time criss-crossing the town in search of Jimmy, so she said, "You know what? I think I'll drop by the library. Catch you later."

She barely got through the door before the librarian at the front desk pointed at the sign that said NO SHOES NO ENTRANCE. She went down to the beach where she saw a couple of kids she knew.

"Flops," she said, "I need flops or the Hag from Hell won't let me dig in the books." Shirley let her borrow her flops. They weren't shoes but they would keep her skin from contaminating the carpets.

HH had great red talons that she used to guard the books like they were her own children. One time, Frances had been deep in thought, wondering about the end of the universe or something and HH had noticed that she was sitting with her book upside down. She said something snide and Frances said, "I'm dyslexic. All the letters are upside down and backwards. I have to read this way." Her mother had heard about that, too. That was the trouble with being related to most of the town. Everyone was a cousin or second cousin or third cousin twice removed. There was no privacy.

"It puts bread and butter on the table," her mother had said. "How do you think I get the listings?"

Frances wondered if the librarian was a relative of some kind. It was a frightening thought. She wore a wig that looked like it had been used for dusting the furniture.

"I'd like," she said in her sweetest voice, "to learn about this area. You know, about my heritage and that sort of thing."

HH grinned at her. Her mouth was a slash of violent red. Her cheeks each had a circle of rouge. She smelled of lavender and dust.

"Local histories," she said and led the way. On her arm were thirteen bangles. "This is the best place to start." She pulled some huge books off the shelf and handed them to Frances.

One was the history of Eddyville. Some of it read like tourist bumpf—the golden sands and blue skies kind of stuff—but most of it was to the point. It had been written by locals and it was jammed with family histories.

Frances thumbed through the pages, stopped with a sense of shock when she saw a picture of her mother, then realized it wasn't her mother. It was her gran when she was younger. There was also an elderly woman in a long dress with her hair piled up on her head.

Then there was a picture of Frances. But it couldn't be her. She looked at the publication date. It was before she was born. She looked at the picture again, and now she knew it wasn't her because the girl was in peysufot.

She checked a note at the bottom of the page. It was Ingibjorg. It made her dizzy, though. How could this sort of stuff be sitting all this time out in public and she didn't know anything about it? There was a list of people in her family. Her father wasn't included. The book had been published before her mother got married.

"Could I please have a pencil and some paper," she said to HH. "I'd like to make some notes."

"If you wanted," the librarian said, "we could just duplicate whatever pages you need. It's ten cents a page."

Frances searched in her pockets.

"That's all right," HH said. "No one will know."

Maybe, Frances thought, HH actually has a name. She'd have to check.

As she left, she felt she had a treasure. All this material to add to the family tree. She was going to be a genealogical detective. She was going to accumulate the evidence. She wasn't sure what it was going to be evidence of. Maybe her father had been murdered. Maybe that's why everything was such a big secret.

When they were duplicating the pages, HH held one up. She pointed at Ingibjorg's picture.

"That's a good picture of Runa," she said.

"Ingibjorg," Frances corrected her.

"When my mother talked about her, she always called her by her middle name, Runa. It means someone who knows and keeps secrets. She was good at that."

9

Back at the cottage, Frances took a fresh sheet of paper and printed her great-great-grandparents' names at the top. She drew a line down from the middle. There were fifteen children. Three of them died as kids from measles and whooping cough. Still, it was no wonder she was related to half the world. She had to start over.

She taped two pages together and worked across them. Bigger paper, she thought. I'm going to need humungous paper.

No wonder so many people in town looked like her in some way. Same ears on this one, same hair on that one, same nose on that one. No wonder she had to work so hard to be herself. No wonder going to town was such a strain. Looking at bits and pieces of yourself on someone else was difficult. Give me back my nose. Those are my eyes. Surrender those ears. Her gran was always saying that's cousin so-and-so and second cousin so-and-so and third cousin so-and-so until she'd put her hands over her ears and refused to listen.

All at once, she stopped. She felt like ice water was trickling down her back. Her arms were covered in goose bumps. She'd felt like this sometimes when she'd wake up from a nightmare in which she thought someone was standing over her bed. Right now, she was sure someone was watching over her shoulder.

She couldn't move.

"Go away," she said. She shut her eyes. "Go away."

Just then Gran came through the door to tell her supper was ready.

"All right," Gran said. "If that's the way you feel."

"No, no! I wasn't talking to you. I was just talking to myself." She slid off her stool. She turned and looked. Nothing but the walls and her big teddy bear stared back at her from the bed.

"You all right?" Gran asked, looking her over.

"Fine. Just daydreaming, I guess. Must have dozed off. Must be the heat." She followed her gran into the kitchen. Her mother was putting a vase of bulrushes and black-eyed Susans on the table. Her cellular was beside her water glass.

"Emily, I'm putting together this history of the family," Frances said. "I figured it'd be neat to get pictures of everyone, and birth certificates and marriage licenses and stuff and put them underneath. It's going to be humungous. I'm going to use an eight-by-four sheet of that white wallboard that's sitting in the garage. Won't that be great?"

Her mother suddenly looked haggard and in disarray. It was like watching thin plastic melt when it was left too close to the stove.

She leaned one hand on the table and said, "I think I'll lie down. Go ahead without me." When she saw their looks of concern, she said, "I haven't been sleeping well. Maybe I've been overdoing it a bit."

Frances wondered if she'd been having too many tea cups full of gin and tonic but, later, after they'd had their pita bread and Greek salad, she surreptitiously checked the bottle. It was nearly full.

Her mother slept for two hours. It was completely uncharacteristic of her unless she had a migraine. When she did get up, instead of rushing away, she paced around, standing up and sitting down any number of times.

Finally, she said, "I've got to go out for a walk. This place is too crowded."

"Weird," Frances said. She was clipping people's heads out of one of the pictures she'd copied at the library and pasting them onto the names on her genealogy chart. "I wonder if I'll get like that when I'm older."

"You could end up like me, instead," Gran said.

Frances had a vision of herself dressing up in old-fashioned clothes and singing off-key in front of television cameras, chaining herself to heritage trees, having a boyfriend with a bad haircut whose chompers weren't his own.

A raging granny in love. It was too much for her.

"Don't do that to me, Gran," she said. "I can't handle it right now."

The strange thing was, she, too, felt as if the cottage was crowded, as if throngs of people were trying to get her attention. Ever since she could remember, that feeling had come and gone. Pretend playmates, her gran had called them when she'd sit for hours serving cups of tea and cookies from her Barbie tea set. Gradually, she'd given up the pretend playmates for real ones but sometimes, like now, it was as if the air was thick with memories of them, as if the air was trying to engage her in interesting, confusing conversations in a language she no longer understood.

She took the canoe and retreated to the marsh. In the heat, even the frogs were silent. She pushed herself along the canal with a single stroke, let the canoe glide until it had nearly stopped, then lightly dug the paddle into the black water. The level of the lagoon had fallen and hummocks of brown, rotting reeds rose from the water. Above them new cattails grew.

She thought about fishing but she knew if she caught anything here, it would be small, bony pike with amber flesh that tasted of mud. Bubbles of gas from the rotting vegetation rose randomly to the surface and broke.

She eased into a small harbor. A group of mallards swam lazily away from the canoe. During the hunting season, they'd scramble into the reeds, but now they were content to stay a paddle's length away.

Dead and living willow were mixed together along the water. There was a small dock. It looked like the ideal swimming hole but none of them ever swam here because of the bloodsuckers. She stayed away from the willows because they were filled with mosquitoes. She looked at the dark water. If the canoe tipped and she drowned, they would easily find her. There was no current here.

When she'd risked asking her mother about where her father had disappeared, her mother had said, "North," in a way that discouraged asking anything more.

Too much silence, Frances thought. In the past the marsh had been a refuge. Any time anything went wrong she could go there, could spend her time with the birds and muskrats. Now it wasn't helping.

This is nuts, she told herself. What's the matter with me? Why can't I be like everyone else?

She paddled back, then fled to town on her bicycle, pedaling as fast as she could, almost skidding on the graveled, washboard road. She knew the penalty for losing control. She'd end up with scraped arms and legs, long patches of scabs. Her mother wouldn't have any sympathy for her. She was always preaching about keeping control over your behavior and not letting your emotions run away with you.

Out on the highway she pedaled like fury. She stayed away from the pioneer road and stuck to the asphalt. Let's roll, she thought, the speed of light, faster than a speeding bullet.

She braked as she turned down Main Street. To her relief she saw Wendy and Bryan. Then she realized that Jimmy was with them. That meant they'd all get to admire his hair. If Wendy had her way, she'd spend all summer watching him comb it while she repeated everything he said.

They weren't really doing anything. They'd been down to the dock but the fish weren't biting and Wendy wasn't keen on the beach since she'd got a sunburn the day before.

"Why," Frances said before she could stop herself, "don't we head for the family farm? You've never been there, have you? There's all sorts of stuff from pioneer days. The great-greats lived out there." Why, she asked herself, did I say that?

To her surprise, they all thought it was a good idea. They filled up their water bottles at the fountain.

All the way there, even when they stopped to eat saskatoons and raspberries from bushes at the side of the road, she felt this terrible tug of war, as if she were being pulled in two different directions. They rode four abreast so no one had to eat dust. The poplar trees drooped in the heat.

She was relieved when she saw there were no ravens on the barn roof.

"Great place," Jimmy said when they reached the gate. Frances wasn't sure whether he meant it or not. The way the dust was going to react to the gel in his hair, he wasn't going to be able to get a comb through it. It would be like concrete.

Just as she thought this, he took out his flip-out comb, flipped it out and ran it through his hair. She could see it was a struggle.

"Why," she asked, "are you always combing your hair?"

To her surprise, Jimmy did not take umbrage (she loved umbrage—it was a word she hardly ever got to use) at her question. He just kept combing and said, "You've seen my dad, right?"

She nodded.

"How much hair has he got?"

She thought about it a second. "None."

"That's right," Jimmy agreed. "Nada. None. He's got more hair in one ear than on his whole head. That's going to be me in a few years. I'm enjoying my hair while I can."

They all stood there, holding onto their bikes, contemplating what he'd look like completely bald. Wendy had a sort of shocked look.

"You get your hair from your mother, not your father," Frances replied. "It's genetic."

Jimmy's hand froze halfway through a stroke. He was immobilized. His entire system had crashed.

"Re-boot," Frances said. "Control Alt Delete."

His hand jerked, then he took the comb out of his hair.

"You're kidding," he said.

"Read it in a biology book." He looked unsure. "I also read it in Ann Landers."

He looked relieved. AL was the real authority.

"My mom," he said, sounding pleased. She had masses of hair. He put his comb in his pocket. He started to smile—not at Frances, not at Wendy, not at Bryan, but at something inside, something he was seeing for the first time. "Yay, Mom."

They pushed open the gate, then wheeled their bikes onto the property. The only sound was their feet on the grassy path, but Frances felt like she was in the midst of a tumult, as if many people were all trying to talk to her at once.

Stop it, she thought. Right now. Or I'm going home.

It stopped, just like that. All at once she could hear the crickets as they jumped about in random arcs.

Assertiveness, she thought, is good.

They explored the old cabin. At first the floor had been packed dirt, she knew. Then there had been planks her great-great had shaped by hand with an adz. Most of the floor had rotted away or been pushed apart by the saplings that now grew inside the walls. In the corners there were still pieces of the planks. She showed the others the marks from the adz.

"I wonder," Bryan said, breaking his code of silence, "what it was like to cut down the trees, haul them here, then square them off by hand? Like imagine doing that today. Sweat a lot?" He knelt down and rubbed his thumb over the surface of the wood.

Square them off, Frances noted. She didn't think he'd know a fact like that. For a long time she'd thought he was practicing to join some religious order that didn't allow talking. She'd only had Wendy's word for it that he could have a conversation more than one word long. That's why she thought he didn't like her much. Or figured she was too much of a kid to bother talking to.

"Wouldn't it be great," Jimmy said, "if we found buried treasure or something."

"Buried treasure," Wendy repeated.

Frances was going to quote her gran about how her great-greats hadn't even had two pennies to rub together, then thought better of it. If she wanted them to stay, she needed to let them have their own fantasies.

They followed her into the barn. They explored the stalls. All they found was the metal part from a pitchfork. They climbed into the loft. She showed them where she had found the trunk. There were still bits and pieces of farm machinery lying about. They hauled them to the door and dropped them to the ground.

"I heard," Jimmy said, "that farmers used to put their savings in glass jars and bury them. We should have a metal detector."

"Metal detector," Wendy repeated.

Before the summer was over, Frances realized, they would swear undying devotion, buy matching jackets. If they stayed together, they would turn into one of those old couples who looked like twins. Same clothes, same walk, same attitude. There were all sorts of them who stayed at the hotel. Mr. and Mrs. Identical. It was a terrifying thought.

The windows of the farmhouse were boarded up. The doors were nailed shut. Frances knew they could get in through the wood chute. There was a small door that she'd called the elf's door when she was little. It was a real door with a handle, but it was only about two feet square.

They had to go in feet first, then flip onto their stomachs and let themselves down to the basement floor. They ended up in the wood bin. The basement wasn't a real basement but more of a square hole that held a furnace and served as a root cellar.

There were two small windows set into the basement walls. Shafts of sunlight filtered through the spaces between the boards on the windows. There were only four stairs and then the door into the kitchen. Green paint was peeling off the walls. The floor was covered in dust. They looked in the cupboards and tried the hand pump that was bolted into place beside the sink. Frances showed them the parlor and the bedrooms. There was still an old couch and overstuffed chair in the parlor but the bedrooms were empty. When they moved about, the sound was magnified.

Something, something, she kept thinking as they moved from room to room. There had been a potbellied stove but Uncle Ben had hauled it away to decorate his rec room.

They had returned to the kitchen when Jimmy found a piece of paper in one of the drawers.

"What is it?" she asked.

"Nothing," he said in disgust. "It's not even English." He threw the paper down.

Something, something, she thought and went to look.

She recognized it right away. It was a sheet cut out of the diary. She picked it up. It was the same looping, curving writing. Except this sheet wasn't moldy.

"What is it?" Wendy asked when she saw the look on Frances's face.

"Just some old writing. It's in Icelandic. I'll show it to my gran." She stuffed the sheet into the front of her shirt.

"Look at this!" Bryan exclaimed. A piece of board was propped in one corner. He held it up for them to see. "Square nails. These are handmade. Can I take them?"

Frances shrugged. "Why not?"

Bryan wiggled them loose. When they got outside, he showed them the flat heads and flat sides of the nails.

"The only place I've seen handmade nails before is in the museum," he said.

They were standing beside the barbed wire fence. Frances reached out and plucked some wool from one of the barbs. As soon as she did that, she felt light-headed, the way she sometimes felt when she got off one of the rides at the fair.

Something, something, echoed through her head on the way back. Not loud and noisy but quiet and knowing, like she'd found the answer to a secret.

Jimmy left them at the road to the island. "He's really happy," Wendy said. "About his hair, I mean. Imagine. He's been worried about what was going to happen to his hair and never told anyone. And all along, he had nothing to worry about."

"Yeah," Frances replied. She thought it would be too cruel to explain the rest of the equation. The mother just passed on the gene. She got it from her father. That was Jimmy's grandfather. He was bald, too.

Fate, she thought, has a terrible sense of humor.

10

When Frances got home, she hurried into her room and put the diary page on her desk. She studied the page closely, then turned away.

As she did, she realized that two of the words said *my friends*.

She stopped absolutely still. If the room had burst into fire, she couldn't have moved.

I can't read Icelandic, she thought. I know I can't. But the words had been absolutely clear.

The hair on the back of her neck stood up. Slowly, she turned and looked again. The Icelandic was unreadable again. She breathed a sigh of relief.

Then, when she wasn't concentrating, another word jumped out at her. *Cows*.

How did she know it was cows? She went over to the bed and lay down. I've lost it, she thought. I think I can do something I can't. Sometimes she dreamt she could fly and sometimes, even after she woke up, she still felt like she could fly. She'd even tried jumping off the roof of the cottage in winter, but there'd been a snowdrift to fall into when flapping her arms didn't work.

It's like the flying, she thought. I'm just being over-imaginative, not connected to reality. She could hear her mother's voice saying, "Get connected to reality."

If we had cable TV, I'd sit and watch Wheel of Fortune or something, she thought. Something to get me back to reality.

The trouble was she had recognized some of the words, or thought she did.

It wasn't possible, she thought. It was as if she had been looking at Chinese characters with no understanding of what they meant, then a moment later they revealed themselves to her and she could read them. Or Greek. Or Russian. One moment a mystery and the next a familiar language.

She heard her mother's bedroom door slam. She wasn't going to tell anyone else about this. They thought she was odd anyway. They'd be hauling her off to doctors who would give her pills and then send her to see a shrink. She'd be treated like one of those people who claimed they were Cleopatra or Napoleon.

Maybe people had language programs in their head. All the languages in the world were there and something stimulated the right one, like hearing your parents talking Hungarian would open up the Hungarian one. How else would kids all over the world learn different languages?

She decided she'd bike down to the Greek restaurant and see if there were more packages waiting to be triggered. Maybe I'm a natural polyglot and don't know it, she thought. It would be great to have people say at parties, she's a polyglot. However, when she got to the Greek restaurant and stood in front of a Greek sign and waited for enlightenment to occur, nothing happened. The Greek words stayed Greek.

◆

The next day, when Frances went to visit TOG, he was in the library. He asked her to push him to the dining room.

The room was nearly full. There was the clatter of dishes. Everyone stopped talking and stared when Frances and TOG sat at a table. Then they all leaned slightly forward and the buzz of conversation started again.

When they were settled, TOG ordered coffee for both of them. He's not treating me like a kid, Frances thought.

"Chocolate cake or vinarterta with your coffee?" he asked.

"Vinarterta," she immediately replied. "We never

get it unless someone gives us a piece. My mom says it takes too much time to make." It was time, she thought, to elevate him from TOG. He'd be Mr. J. now.

Mr. J. smiled approvingly. He asked her if she liked skyr, rullupylsa, mysuostur, kleinur. She happily said yes to skyr and kleinur, but she made a face at rullupylsa and mysuostur.

He laughed. "I like the rullupylsa," he said, "but not mysuostur. When I was a boy someone offered it to me on brown bread and I thought it was peanut butter. I couldn't offend my host so I had to eat the whole slice." He made a face and shook his head.

When the coffee came, he poured some into his saucer to cool, put a lump sugar between his teeth and sucked the coffee through the sugar.

"It's called saucering," he said, looking around defiantly. "Queen Victoria did it and so did all the Icelanders at one time. Here, put the lump sugar between your teeth. Get a good hold. These aren't ordinary cubes. Ordinary cubes break. This is special hard sugar. Now, slurp the coffee through the sugar."

Frances sipped her coffee from her cup. Then, feeling rather daring, she poured some into her saucer and imitated Mr. J.

"Are you teaching her bad habits?" one of the waitresses asked as she put down two dessert plates with vinarterta on them. Mr. J. held up two fingers, then pointed at Frances.

"Young people can handle more than one piece," he said. "Give her one iced and one un-iced. Then she can decide where she stands on the great debate."

Frances was pleased because she knew what he was talking about. There were the icers and the non-icers. Each group claimed their way of making vinarterta was the right way.

She counted the layers of cake. "Seven," she said. The layers were thin, the way they were supposed to be, with mashed prunes alternating with the pastry.

She gave Mr. J. the original sheet from the day before. He glanced at it, then put it aside. He read her what he had already translated.

"After we left Montreal there was nothing but wilderness. There are about thirty Icelanders. There's been no sign of the stowaway. Then, on the third day, I looked out the train window. It was just at dusk and there was a face looking at me. I turned around thinking it was the reflection of a boy standing in the aisle but no one was there. When I turned back, the image was gone.

"'What is it now?' my aunt demanded. She had no patience with me. If we'd been alone, she'd have slapped me or pulled my hair.

"I pointed at the window.

"'Trees,' she said. 'Nothing but trees. How will your father clear enough land for sheep?'

"There are no trees in Iceland. Before the trip began, none of us had ever been farther than the farm that Gunnar's family owned. To get there we had to walk most of a day. I'd only once seen a non-Icelander. He was an Englishman who came to study birds. Now there are non-Icelanders everywhere. Talking in a language I do not understand. Gunnar has been helping me learn English with his dictionary. Every day we memorize ten words. He does not want to go to the colony. He is determined to stay in Winnipeg so he can become a teacher."

"That's all," Mr. J. said. "I'm afraid that I won't be here tomorrow. I've got to visit the hospital. I'd rather be having ice cream with you. Do you think you might be able to find some more of these pages? While I'm away, you could look for them. I'm just staying overnight. Got to get my ticker running on time again."

11

::
::

"I hear she's been volunteering at the old folks' home," her mother said. She had an hour between clients. "I didn't know she had it in her."

"That so?" her gran replied. "Never said anything to me, either. You'd think when she decided to do something thoughtful and kind, she'd let us know."

"If she's taking care of that Mr. Johannson, I hope she doesn't believe everything he tells her."

"I was learning saucering today," Frances said. She hated it when they talked about her as if she wasn't there. "That's how I'm going to drink my coffee from now on."

She made a hasty exit. She'd just returned to get a snack and a bottle of water. Mr. J. had said to get those papers.

When she got to the farmhouse, she propped her bike against the back wall, pried the boards off the two basement windows, then let herself in through the wood chute. The basement was dank and musty. She waited, listening. The only sound was of mice scampering in the walls.

She turned on her flashlight and methodically played the beam over the basement. There was the old furnace that looked like an octopus, its arms rising to the floor above. She checked some dusty wooden shelves. All they held were a few canning jars.

Now that she was inside, coming by herself didn't seem like such a good idea.

She crept up the stairs one at a time, stepping, then pausing, not sure what she was listening for. She pushed open the basement door. If anything moved, she was going to jump out of her skin.

She went to the kitchen. She looked in the cupboards.

She was on her knees with her head stuck in the cupboard when she heard a voice whisper, "Frances."

The hair stood up on the back of her neck. She remained rigid. She was expecting someone to touch her but nothing happened. Slowly, she moved back and looked over her shoulder.

No one was there. When her heart quit pounding, she went back to her search.

She opened the rest of the cupboards. They were empty and the wall was blank.

She ran the light over the room. The walls were a

pale green, with the upper part covered in yellow wallpaper with a pink flower pattern. Black pipes hung from some copper wire. There was a pile of soot underneath them.

She paused, forcing herself to relax. When she did, she thought of the Purloined Letter. It was one of her favorite stories. In it, a letter was stolen and then hidden in the most obvious place—so obvious no one thought of looking there.

That made her look at the room once more. There was battleship linoleum on the floor. There was the ceiling. There were the blank walls. That left the cupboards.

She wished she had a ladder. She opened a lower door, braced herself on it and climbed onto the counter.

Nothing, nothing, she said to herself as she played her light over the shelves.

It was when she got down that she thought she saw someone through the door to the parlor. She flashed her light there but once again there was nothing. Determined not to be frightened, she strode into the room.

The faded, wine-colored couch and chair were covered in dust. Three pictures hung on the wall. They weren't anything special—just prints cut from magazines and put into frames.

She took them down one after the other. She looked at the backs. Brown paper was glued over two of them but the third one was covered with a sheet from the diary. There was no way to lift it off without tearing it, so she took the picture with her and quickly hurried down the stairs and climbed outside. Back in the sunlight, she breathed a sigh of relief.

She put the picture in her knapsack, then turned.

"Who are you?" she said before she could help herself. There were just the thistles and long grass. Even the crickets were silent.

Suddenly, the stillness was broken by the beat of wings. A black raven swooped up over the barn, stalled in mid flight and dropped neatly onto the ridge.

Muninn, she breathed.

The raven bobbed its head and strutted along the roof's crest. Frances took a sandwich out of her knapsack, unwrapped it, then held it out. The raven stopped prancing and leaned forward as if to get a better look. She threw the sandwich toward the barn. It fell into the long grass.

The raven gave a harsh cry, swooped down in a steep glide, passed the sandwich, then made a sharp, hooking turn, stalled and dropped into the grass. In a moment it rose, its wings beating.

Safely back on the roof, it dropped the sandwich,

put its foot on the bread and began to tear off pieces and swallow them.

"What do you have to tell me?" Frances whispered. The black raven leaned forward, as if it were going to speak. Her head began to fill with noise—dark static that made no sense.

At that moment, someone yelled from down the road. It was Bryan.

He waved. She walked over to him.

"What are you doing here?" she asked.

He held out a bucket. There was a mixture of saskatoons and raspberries.

"My mother said if I got enough for a pie, she'd bake one. I remembered there were lots here. You want to help me pick?"

They worked their way along the edge of the bush. Bryan pulled down the saskatoon bushes so that they could get the best berries from the top. They shared a drink from her water bottle.

"You and Wendy both like Jimmy, eh?" he said.

Frances's jaw shut with surprise. Bryan was busy picking twigs and leaves out of his berry bucket. He was not a meticulous picker.

Frances didn't reply and Bryan laughed nervously, then took something out of his pocket. He held out his hand.

"I've made rings out of three of those nails. I gave

Wendy hers. I thought you might like one. After all, they're your nails."

"The Three Mouseketeers," she said. "All for cheese and cheese for all."

"I'd like," he said, "to do an essay on your family's log cabin for our school paper. Would it be okay if I came out one day and took pictures? I could interview you. I mean, if you wouldn't mind." He started to get flustered. "I sort of think I'd like to be a journalist. I mean, you know." He looked at his hands. "I thought I could do a story about the cabin and then maybe another one about the nails. Ordinary things can be really interesting."

She hadn't heard him talk this much in a whole summer. He turned bright red and stopped talking.

Frances had seen him taking pictures. He was always carrying a camera, but he'd never said anything about wanting to be a journalist.

"Want to race back?" she asked.

"Okay," he replied. He looked relieved. All the talking was obviously a strain.

"You're taller," she said. She pressed her hip against his. Then, using her thumb and index finger, she measured the difference between the top of their hipbones.

She held up her fingers to show him the difference. "You've got longer legs than me. That means I get a handicap."

He laughed and pressed his left hand to his cheek. It was a gesture he used when he was embarrassed.

"Okay. I'll count to five."

She jumped on her bike and tried to spin away, but the gravel made her slide sideways.

"One," he yelled. She was getting her balance, trying to get to where the gravel had been pushed away. "Two, three." She was pedaling as hard as she could. "Four, five."

She glanced over her shoulder. He was on his bike and riding as hard as he could. She jerked her bike up and over the railway tracks, turned hard onto the asphalt highway. He yelled and she could tell he was gaining on her.

I should have made him count to ten, she thought, as she turned onto the mud road through the swamp. The road was filled with ruts. On either side were ditches. If she wiped out, it was going to be scab city.

She got caught in a rut, jerked up her front wheel, then was out of it. She knew she was kicking up a lot of dust. He'd be choking on it.

There was no way to avoid the washboard. The bike and her bones rattled so hard, she thought she'd fall apart. She did better on the rough patches but he did better on the straight stretches. She could hear him right behind her.

Just before they got to the cottage she hit another stretch of washboard. If she slowed down even for one foot-stroke, he'd pass her. The front wheel of her bike bounced up. She leaned against it but the choppiness threw her front wheel higher.

She tried to hold the wheel straight. It dropped into a tight rut that twisted the handlebars sideways. She felt herself lifting up over the handlebars. She let go and as she turned head over heels, she knew the bike was following her. She hoped it wasn't going to land on top of her.

She hit the water with a force that drove her to the bottom. She scrambled up, spitting and shaking her head. The green algae that grew in layers on the surface was wrapped around her like a coat. She swung her arms and her body. The algae made plopping sounds as it dropped into the water. She pulled the green slime off her head.

"Are you okay?" Bryan asked. He was standing at the edge of the ditch.

Just then a car horn beeped. She looked up. Dr. and Mrs. Skillings were driving by. Mrs. Skillings was smiling and waving at Bryan. When she saw Frances, her hand froze.

"Never mind my mother," Bryan said. "Are you hurt?"

"No," Frances replied. She was going to pull her

bike out of the water when she noticed the strap of her pack. The picture was in the packsack.

She lunged for it, grabbed the handle and thrashed her way out of the water. Her shoes made wet, sloppy sounds. She knelt down and unzipped her pack. Water sloshed around inside.

The picture was soaked. Her heart sank.

12

When she got back to the cottage, her gran said, "Whew! Go change your clothes. What have you been doing? Swimming in the swamp?"

Frances nodded and backed into the bathroom. She showered, then put her clothes in the washing machine.

When she was respectable again, she slipped into her bedroom. The picture was nearly dry. She was relieved to see that the words, although blurred, were still readable. She got out her pocket knife and cut into the wood. Carefully, she chipped the wood away.

The trouble was, she recognized some of the words, or thought she did. It said, she realized, *There are*, then a word she didn't know, then *mountains*.

She tried to relax. Don't panic, she thought, just let it happen. Whatever is going to happen is going to happen. Like her gran said about being kidnapped by aliens. No use going for walks along the road at night when things are flashing across the sky and then panic if somebody hauls you into a space ship.

The next day she wished Mr. J. wasn't at the hospital. She wanted him to see the page. She wouldn't even have minded buying him an ice-cream cone.

She got herself a glass of lemonade and sat outside under the birch trees. The lake was pale blue, absolutely flat. The leaves of the trees drooped. Usually, there was a breeze from the lake that kept the mosquitoes to the west side of the cottage. If she sat still, they'd take it as an invitation to have a drink of their own. She got the shovel and began excavating.

It was a strange and difficult place to have built a grand house. There had long been a road but most of the time, according to her gran, it had been under water. A dyke had only been built in the last thirty years and a road built on top of that. Then a causeway was built, closing the channel between the island and the mainland. The road had been continued on the causeway. The settlers had originally landed on this sandbar and, after one night, began to move their possessions north toward higher, more stable ground where there was protection from the elements. There would have been no neighbors. There was little ground for grazing. There were no fields for farming. The lagoon provided a good harbor but any fish caught would have to be transported to the settlement.

She uncovered the entire length of the footing. The house must have been large because the footing ran ten feet beyond the south end of the cottage. She wished she had a picture of this house that had stood looking forward and back over both lake and lagoon.

She began to dig inside the footing. She turned up a layer of ash and a barely recognizable nail. In places there were just pockets of rust.

She saw the point of something sticking out of the sand. She got down on her knees and began to dig with her hand.

A piece of china came free. She turned it over on her palm. It was yellow with a piece of a black pattern on it. She found nine pieces. When she arranged them on the sand, she had most of a dinner plate. It was quite elegant, with a black border and gold-colored flowers. She took the pieces inside, cleaned them off, then glued them in place.

This wasn't so different from what an archeologist did, she realized. They found pottery fragments and from them learned all sorts of things about whole societies.

She heard her gran come in. The door slammed. That meant something was up. She never slammed the door unless someone was doing something they shouldn't.

Gran was one of the Raging Grannies. She and a group of her friends regularly dressed up in old-fashioned clothes and held protests. They'd mounted the barricades over saving the wood duck, moving the pioneer cemetery, keeping the library, stopping the demolition of the oldest church in town. They'd chained themselves to the old brick post office but that hadn't done any good. The government had hauled them away in a police van and knocked the building down with a bulldozer. Frances was embarrassed every time she saw her gran nose to nose with the local RCMP officer or the mayor or some local businessman.

"They've done it now," Gran shouted. "That's it. We're going to war."

Frances checked the horizon for nuclear explosions. China, Russia, Iraq? she wondered. Desert Storm II?

"The municipal council has approved subdividing the island into fifty-foot lots. They don't care about the marsh. They don't know anything about wetlands."

"They can't do that," Frances said. "I mean, the island is the island. It's a beach. You can't turn it into a subdivision." She was thinking about the frogs.

"Greed," Gran spat. "It's always the same. It doesn't matter how good something is. Someone will wreck it in order to make money."

"What about the muskrats and the fish? And the pelicans?"

"And they'll bring cats. They'll let them run wild. It'll be the end of the birds."

"Maybe Emily could talk to somebody."

"Your mother is part of it. She's known about it all along. She wants to be the exclusive agent for selling the lots."

Frances's heart sank. Her mother was obsessed with success. She constantly worried about money, but they had more than enough to live on. Her gran had the insurance policy from when her husband died. If her mother just quit shopping all the time, they'd need very little to live on. It was like she had to prove that she could afford things—a new car, new clothes, new furniture.

There's something crazy driving her, Frances thought, and now she wants to take where we live and carve it up so she can make more money.

Her mother arrived about an hour later. Frances thought there'd be a lot of yelling. Instead, there was an icy exchange. Her gran swore that she'd lie in the middle of the road rather than let construction equipment through. Emily said it was progress.

Change isn't always progress, Gran replied. They'd had that argument before.

Frances didn't want to get caught in the middle so she stayed out of it. When everything was quiet, she said, "Have you got a picture of my dad somewhere? I'd like to have it for my genealogy chart."

"Not right now, Frances," her mother shouted. "I've got enough to deal with."

◆

The next morning Frances slipped outside to sit in one of the wooden lawn chairs. The air was alive with dragonflies. There were the large purple ones, smaller red ones, but mostly golden ones.

As she sat with her glass of iced tea, the golden dragonflies began to land on her. They landed on her hair, on her shoulders, on her chest and back, on her arms. She sat there covered in golden bodies and wings.

This is the kind of gold I want, she thought. She had done this every summer since she could remember. The dragonflies settled on the edge of her glass, on the backs of her hands. This was what the island and the lagoon were all about. When she sat like this, she felt like she wasn't just her, separate, but part of something bigger. It was what made her not afraid of the frogs and garter snakes, why she had learned to whistle the sour-sweet song of the red-winged blackbird.

The sun had just risen and its rays reflecting off the dragonflies enclosed her in a golden aura. After a time, she carefully stood up and lightly shook herself. The dragonflies reluctantly lifted away.

13

Frances walked to town. When there was conflict and turmoil she found that walking helped her calm down. The wind was from the east so the lake was high. She had to walk close to the ragged edge of grass. Here, many of the trees were stunted from growing in sand. Their trunks were pitted and black where branches had died.

Normally she loved walking the beach, but this time she looked at the line of poplars and the grass and thought, It isn't going to be like this much longer. There'll be houses jammed one beside the other.

She'd seen it happen to other beaches. The cottages were torn down. Big houses were jammed onto the lots. People brought in sod and created yards. The native trees were bulldozed and replaced with a few ornamentals.

Why, she wondered, did people come to live on places like the island if they were going to turn it into another suburban development? Ahead of her sand-pipers were running up and down the water's edge. Every so often, they'd lift briefly into a gust of wind, then settle.

Mr. J. was waiting for her. His face looked strained and pale but he insisted on a strawberry cone.

"I feel irritable," he said. "It's got nothing to do with you. It's part of growing old and not feeling well. If I could walk around, even if I had to use one of those walkers, it wouldn't be so frustrating. I don't want to sit here. Push me to the dock. I haven't been there for a long time."

The dock looked like a rainbow had broken up over it. In spite of the gusting wind, the tourists in their bright clothes were so thick that Frances at times had to stop and wait for an opening so they could move forward. The finger docks were jammed with sailboats.

"When I was a boy," Mr. J. said, "there was nothing but fishing boats here. We used to make wages helping unload the freighters that brought in the fish from the north. Ten cents an hour. Doesn't sound like much but then this cone would have only cost a nickel. We used to just about live on this dock. Fishing for perch and swimming when we couldn't get the odd job to do. Push me right out to the end. I want to see the lake with nothing in the way."

He sat at the end of the dock for ten minutes, not saying anything. Frances sat with her feet over the water. The surface was an opaque green at this time of year but in the spring, just after the ice went out from shore, she was able to see right to the bottom. The water would be so transparent, it seemed barely a foot deep, but it really was over twenty.

She told him about finding the page and feeding the raven. She also told him about the dunking in the marsh. He held the page up to the sunlight.

"Don't fret," he said, "about what is done. It's a waste of time and energy. Besides, think how symbolic it is. Present concerns are always obscuring the past."

"Like sub-dividing the island," she answered.

He shrugged. "A lot of people aren't long-headed. They live for today."

"I don't want to be like that."

"Then you won't be," he replied as he put down the page. "It sounds like you soon will have house ravens. You will have to be firm with them. They can be very demanding. The ravens reward those who treat them well. They are very intelligent but they are great thieves. You won't want to leave out anything shiny that you value or it will find its way to their rook."

"I feel," she said, deciding to risk sounding silly, "like they have a message for me."

"Then you must listen carefully. It is not the telling that usually is at fault. It is the listening."

"You don't think I'm strange because I think that birds might have a message for me?"

"No stranger than the North American natives, the Vikings, the Greeks, nearly every culture except of course today's scientific culture that has an answer for nearly everything and knows nothing."

That made her feel better. She was so used to being thought of as odd that she'd begun to think of herself as odd.

Suddenly, she said, "Do you know my mom?"

Mr. J. looked at her out of the sides of his eyes, then nodded. "Yes, I do. She sold my house for me."

"I don't mean like that. Did you know her when she was younger?"

He nodded again. Frances was beginning to feel frustrated. Usually he was quite willing to chat. They'd talked about Icelandic horses, volcanoes, mythology, Vilhjalmur Stefansson's explorations in the north, even Halldor Laxness, whom she had never heard of before.

"She was my best grade twelve English student," he said. "Like you, she was a great reader and very smart."

"Me?" Frances said. "Smart?" She'd never thought of herself as smart, only as different. For a moment she felt flattered, then she felt uneasy. She wasn't sure it was such a good idea to be smart. As it was, because she liked words, the kids gave her nicknames like the Brain and Einstein. It was sort of a compliment at times but at other times it wasn't.

"Time for work," Mr. J. said abruptly. "I'm starting to feel tired. After a visit to the hospital, I poop out pretty quickly. If you want to get more of the diary done, then we need to get to it."

She pushed him back to the OFH. They sat in the shade on the front porch. She hoped that when he translated that she would be wrong about the words she had understood. Instead, she was right. It unsettled her and she had to focus hard to write down what he was saying.

"July 9/88. We arrived at Clyde, Scotland. As we got off the boat they were already lifting the horses out of the hold. They had blindfolded the horses so they wouldn't be frightened. As soon as all of us were together, we were herded down the street. It took five hours before we were on the train. None of us had ever seen a train before. Scotland is beautiful. There are farms and forests and pastures. No one has ever seen trees like this. Some people are frightened by the speed of the train. Everything goes past so fast that it is hard to look at anything properly. The cows all look healthy and well fed. It would be a pleasure to milk one of those.

"It took three hours for us to travel to Glasgow. By this time it was dark out but the streets were lit with lamps. It was amazing to see. When we got off the train we had to hurry. It took us four hours to get to the ship. Some people who were very tired, mostly women and children, got left behind. People from the steamship company went looking for them. I stayed between Pabbi and Gunnar. Walking in a hurry over the cobblestones was very hard for Gunnar and by the time we reached the ship his leg was sore and he was tired.

"I saw that boy again. I don't know how he managed to conceal himself among those who walked to the ship or how he got on but I caught a glimpse of him and nudged Gunnar. By the time Gunnar turned to look, there was nothing to see. He humored me, though, and we went looking. Under and in lifeboats, behind the large pipes.

"'He's here,' I said. 'I saw him. He's got a dirty face and torn trousers and no shoes. How will he survive until we get to Canada?'

"The next morning, when no one was watching, I hid a cup of porridge under my cloak. We went up on deck for exercise. I slipped the cup under the canvas of the lifeboat next to where I'd seen him. Later, when I looked, the cup was empty. After that, I put out a cup every day.

"Gunnar says a cat is probably eating it. He has such a scientific mind. If you can't see it, he doesn't believe it exists. His answer for everything is science. No trolls, no goblins, no huldafolk, no giants.

"Do you have more pages?" Mr.J. asked.

Frances shook her head. She told him about going back to the house and how she'd felt.

"They must be there," he replied. "I can't go with you. Isn't there someone you can take? It's always easier to be brave when there are two."

14

When she went home for lunch, the cottage was silent because her gran and Emily weren't talking to each other. Instead, they used her as an intermediary. Her gran said, "Frances, tell your mother that we need milk the next time she's at the store." Her mother said, "Tell your gran that I won't be home for supper. I have to earn our living."

Frances knew there was no point asking her mother any questions when she was behaving like this. She knew her father had disappeared before she was born. But he must have been in town nine months before.

After lunch, she went to the local newspaper office and asked the editor if she could look through the archives. She told him it was for a school genealogy project. She started with July because she was born in May. She worked her way through the obituaries and news stories.

She managed July, August and September before

the editor said he was closing. There was no point asking him for information. He had only been editor for two years.

The next morning she asked Bryan if he'd go to the farm with her. To her surprise, he immediately agreed.

When they arrived at the farm, both ravens were perched on the farmhouse roof. She hadn't forgotten them. She threw some slices of bread with peanut butter up to them. They both started churring and making the dry chopping sound that meant they were pleased.

Once Frances and Bryan were inside they started a methodical search.

After half an hour, Frances was ready to give up.

"The pages could have just been burned or thrown away," she said. She was sitting with her back to the wall, having a drink of water. "Bryan, where are you?"

"In here." He poked his head around the corner. He was standing in the pantry just off the kitchen. He started to say something but she held her finger to her lips.

"Can you hear that?" He nodded. "There, it's stopped," she said. Bryan picked up a board and went back into the pantry.

She heard a scratching sound. "They're on the roof," she said.

She shut her eyes and held up her hand for him to

be quiet. She didn't want him to see her being weird but the birds moving above them filled her head with sound.

"Muninn, Huginn," she whispered. "Talk to me. Tell me what you know."

"You said you've looked everywhere," he called. "Have you tried the attic?"

"Attic," she said. "What attic?"

She went into the pantry and played her flashlight over the ceiling. There was nothing to see.

Bryan reached up with the board, tapped on the ceiling, then pushed. A piece of ceiling moved. She could see that a square door was fitted so carefully into the ceiling that when it was in place, it was almost invisible.

To reach the ceiling, they were going to need something to stand on. They went back to the parlor to look at the chesterfield and chair. Both were too big to get through the pantry door.

Bryan knelt down. "Get onto my shoulders," he said.

Frances hesitated, then climbed up. He stood. She reached up and pushed the door aside. She immediately ducked her head, for the heat and the smell of the ravens were overpowering.

Both ravens were in the attic and they began their raucous cries until the attic echoed and re-echoed with a cacophony of sound. Then she heard them fly away.

She got one hand on an edge, took a deep breath, pulled herself up, got one knee on Bryan's shoulder, caught hold with her other hand and pulled herself into the darkness. The air was so hot she could barely breathe, and the darkness was total except for a beam of light that came from a hole under the eaves. This was the ravens' entrance.

Frances twisted around until her knees were on the studs. Then she leaned down through the hole and asked Bryan for her flashlight.

She played the beam over the ceiling and along the rafters. There was a huge nest. The ravens, she realized, must have been using the attic for years. She looked more closely at the mass of sticks and twigs. It was intertwined with grass and bark and pieces of string and farmer's binder twine. There were, she was relieved to see, no eggs or young.

At first there seemed to be nothing except the nest, but then she noticed a wooden fish box under the eaves. Gingerly, she crawled along the two-by-fours. She didn't want to step between them and have her foot go crashing through the ceiling.

There were two boxes. The first one was filled with old wooden corks the fishermen used on their nets before the plastic ones were invented. In the second box there were objects wrapped in pieces of flowered oilcloth.

When Frances opened the first package, she found heavy brown paper so dry that it cracked as she touched it. Carefully, she lifted out the package and unwrapped it.

There was a thick glass rectangle. She took it to the hole the ravens used for an entrance and exit.

When she held the glass in the beam of sunlight, she saw that she was holding a photographic plate. There was a couple standing side by side. They were all dressed up. The man was in a stiff-looking suit and the woman was in an Icelandic dress.

Frances knew that she was looking at her great-great-grandparents, Ingibjorg and Gunnar. She gently touched the picture and said, "I've been looking all over for you."

She crawled back to the box and rewrapped the photographic plate. She opened another package. Inside were a cup and saucer of the same pattern as the plate she'd unearthed while digging up the foundations of the house that had burnt down.

Finally, she lifted out a large package. It was tied with cotton fishing twine that had grown so weak that it snapped when she gently tugged on it. Inside, there were layers of soft paper.

Then she stopped. She knew what it was. An

Icelandic dress. Ingibjorg's dress. She couldn't bring herself to unwrap it. She folded the paper back into place. She shone her flashlight into the box.

There was a smaller package at one end of the box. When she unwrapped it, out spilled a lot of flat wooden pieces shaped like the needles used to seam on nets. They were the same shape as the top of an ironing board.

Frances picked up one and turned it around in the light. On it was carved what looked like a capital F, except the vertical line continued past the top horizontal bar. The next was like the top of a Y upside down. The third was a line with a triangle attached in the middle. Most, though, didn't look like anything she'd seen before. Beneath that was an embroidered pillow and a white cloth.

She put everything back as she had found it.

Think before you act, her gran was always saying to her. The last time was after she'd fallen into the water jumping from ice floe to ice floe during the spring. The water hadn't been deep but the shock had been considerable. Look before you leap had taken on real meaning after that.

She gently put the dress back, then fitted the lid onto the box.

"Find anything?" Bryan yelled.

"A box of old corks." She crawled back to the opening and dropped one down to him. "You can have that one. Maybe you can do another article about the different kinds of corks the fishermen have used."

She grabbed the sides of the opening and eased herself down. To fit the door into place, she had to kneel on Bryan's shoulders.

As she tried to move from being on her knees, Bryan shuffled and she lost her balance. She reached out and caught one of the shelves. Her hand skidded on shelf paper.

"Move over this way," she said. "Give me the flashlight."

The paper lining the cupboards was brown and brittle with age. She looked more closely. Underneath there was more paper, older paper. Someone had just laid the shelf paper over it. She pulled up the shelf paper and threw it on the floor. She held the flashlight close to the shelf.

There, in front of her, were pages from the diary. She climbed down, then went around the room collecting the pages. She gave a half laugh. It was simple. Paper had been hard to come by and someone had used the pages to line the shelves.

When they got back to the island, she gave Bryan a hug. She didn't care what anyone would say. He'd gone with her when she'd asked. He'd helped her do something she couldn't do herself.

15

....
....

She hated secrets. Now she had all sorts of secrets of her own. She was uncovering some secrets and creating others.

She put the pages under her bed, then went for a swim. When she came back, her mom was sitting in the kitchen.

"You've been looking at the obituaries at the newspaper office," she said.

"Yup," Frances replied. Why should she be surprised? It was impossible to do anything without it being talked about. "I was looking for a picture of my dad. I want it for my genealogy project."

"Frances," her mother said, "there are some things better left alone. Sometimes we think we want to know something and maybe when we get the answer, we really wish we hadn't asked."

Her mother looked disorganized. Her hair wasn't its usual sculpted self. Her makeup seemed overdone. Her clothes weren't absolutely perfectly ironed. It wasn't like she was wearing a yellow blouse with a red skirt and blue shoes or anything, but it might as well have been.

"We weren't married," her mom said. "It was one of those things. He was an artist and he came out from Iceland for the summer. He was staying at our house. I was seventeen. He was thirty. I fell head over heels in love with him."

"And he drowned?"

"No. He went back to Iceland."

Not dead, Frances thought. He's not dead. Then her mind froze. Somewhere distant, someone said, "You guys could have got married, couldn't you?"

She realized that her mother had been crying. Why hadn't she noticed before that her makeup was smudged around her eyes? Everything was moving in slow motion.

"He was already married. He said he was going to go home, get a divorce and come back but, when he got there, he changed his mind."

Frances was thinking about his bones. All those years she'd lain awake at night when the wind blew and the lake pounded on the shore, imagining his bones washing back and forth with the waves. All the years being angry when she thought he might be off in Mexico or Spain going to parties and never thinking about her. All those years of not knowing what to think or how to feel.

"I've got to go outside," she said.

"Frances!" her mother called.

She ran outside. She didn't want her mother following her. She wanted to be alone. She didn't want to have to talk to anyone.

She ran to the dock, undid the line on the canoe and pushed herself into the canal. Her father hadn't drowned so there was no need to be afraid of history being repeated. She paddled hard to where the canal opened into the lagoon, then pushed into open water. The line of trees on the other side formed a tumbled, tempting edge she'd looked at many times.

She dug her paddle into the water. By the time she reached the western edge of the marsh, she was starting to think again. She put her paddle down as the canoe slid among the bulrushes.

Gradually, she became aware of the cars zipping by on the highway. The sound would rise to a crescendo, then fade away. Everyone was rushing somewhere, busy with their own lives. She'd turned toward the lagoon so she could look at the island. They were going to carve it up and turn it into another suburb. They were going to lie and cheat and steal and sit at night counting their money.

Three pelicans glided into view, slipped down the

sky and skidded to a landing on the water. They made her feel better. The pelicans had nearly all disappeared because of the chemicals, but they stopped using the chemicals and now the pelicans were back. She loved the pelicans. They had their own beach where they gathered each day before they left to go fishing. She often watched them with binoculars.

Maybe, she thought, I'll become a biologist and an environmental soldier.

When she returned to the cottage, her mother was lying on the couch. Frances got a can of pop from the fridge and sat down in the armchair beside the couch. There was a long silence. They avoided each other's eyes.

Frances opened her can of pop and took a sip. Tears started to leak out of the corners of her eyes.

It was, she told herself, more relief than anything. She had a real dad, with a name and a history— someone she could find out about.

"Was he a real artist?" she asked.

"Yes. He's had shows in Europe and the U.S."

Her mother was biting her lip. That meant she was trying not to cry, too.

"Why didn't you tell me? It's no big deal. Lots of kids have single mothers. That's why you didn't change your name when you got married. It wasn't because you thought women should keep their own names."

"I'm sorry," her mother said. Frances was shocked. She'd never heard her mother say she was sorry before, about anything.

"Is he still alive?"

Her mother nodded. "I think I need to go lie down," she said. "We can talk about this later."

Frances sat on the floor in front of her great-great-amma's trunk. For awhile she just stared at it. Then she reached out and ran her fingers over the numbers.

Life can be hard, she thought. But this can't be harder than packing all you own into this trunk and moving to a country halfway around the world. Ingibjorg didn't even know the language.

She remembered the picture she'd studied in the attic. When it was taken, Ingibjorg was only a few years older than herself.

Her gran came in and sat down beside her. "Your mother was ashamed. There was a lot of gossip. You know what small towns are like. People aren't always nice. Some pretty cruel things get said by people who should know better."

"She lied," Frances said. "You lied, too. You all knew the truth and you all lied. Aunt Martha and Uncle Ben. Everybody. I don't trust any of you anymore."

"We thought it was a good idea at the time," her gran said. "We always intended to tell you but it never seemed like the right time. People make mistakes."

She handed Frances a piece of paper. "If you'd looked in the newspaper for the week of May 21, you'd have found your birth announcement. We weren't ashamed of you."

Frances took the clipping and read it. *Frances Ingibjorg Sigurdsson, born with great joy at 4 A.M. May 21 in the Eddyville hospital.*

"Your father was very handsome. We were all smitten with him. He was a painter and a writer. He'd traveled all over Europe. Your mother loved literature and he knew all about books and authors. She'd never met anyone like him. Your grandpa Villy and he used to recite the Eddas. They kept trying to top each other. It's not like your mom was some giddy fool. She was hard working, sensible and practical. She still is. Too much so at times. Can you imagine her being silly?"

"When you've taken me to the art gallery, have we seen any of his paintings?"

Her gran shook her head. "He shows in Europe."

"Maybe you're all lying about other things," Frances replied. She knew it was cruel but it was how she felt. There was nothing solid under her feet anymore. "Maybe you're not my gran. Maybe she's not my mother. After all, she never wants me to call her mom. She never wanted me to call you Amma. Maybe nobody's who they say they are."

16

Frances washed her hair and braided it the way her great-great's was in the picture. Then she put on a blouse and skirt. It was as dressed up as she'd been since her mother's Christmas party. Mr. J., she knew, would approve.

She put the pages into her knapsack. She rode to town along the pioneer road. She stopped for a drink at the artesian well.

Nothing had changed but everything had changed. It was like something had shifted and nothing would ever be the same again. Her mother was always going on about Frances not being overcome by her emotions. She had never been sure why she was subjected to these lectures. Now she knew. It wasn't her emotions that were the problem.

"Maybe you won't like the answers you get." Mr. J. had said. He knew about her mother and her dad and had been warning her.

She found him in the library. "I've been waiting," he said. "My heart is set on Cherry Delight."

She showed him the sheaf of pages. She explained where she'd found them. He looked them over. He counted them, then counted the cut stubs of paper in the diary. There were still quite a few missing.

"You've done very well," he said. "You get an A plus for persistence." He began to shuffle through the pages. "These are much better. There's no mold or water damage. You've brought your notebook and pencil."

"My mother told me about my dad," she said. She had to tell someone. "She told me about not being married."

Mr. J. shuffled the papers. She'd noticed that when he was thinking, he liked to do something with his hands.

"They should have told you before." He looked at her sharply and she instantly thought of the ravens. He had a narrow head and sharp nose but it was his eyes most of all that reminded her of Huginn and Muninn. They were the same dark color. "That was the year I retired. I wanted your mother to stay in school. I even offered to tutor her. She was my best student. Some of the parents were opposed. You'd think pregnancy was a communicable disease. Anyway, she wouldn't have any of it. I thought she would take the Governor General's medal. She's very smart."

"Not smart enough not to get pregnant." Frances said it like an accusation. "Then I came along and wrecked things. It's because of me that she had to quit and go to work."

He glared at her. "You're too smart to think like that. Stupid people are entitled to stupid thinking. You are not. She was young and naive. 'I love you' are the most dangerous words in the English language. People shouldn't say them unless they mean them. She didn't know that this sophisticated man was already married. She could have gone to the city and had an abortion. No one would have known. She didn't have to keep you."

"She lied. They lied." She wished that he wasn't in a wheelchair. She wanted to hit him with her fists. She wanted to hit someone.

"Have you never lied for much less serious things than she faced? Do you think five years from now when you are the age she was that you will always tell the truth?"

"It's not my fault," Frances said. As soon as she said it, she couldn't stop the tears. They ran down her face in a stream and they burned like acid. Mr. J. gave her his handkerchief.

When at last the tears stopped, Mr. J. said, "Did

your mother say it was your fault?" She shook her head. "Did your grandmother say it was your fault?" She shook her head again. "It seems to me the only person saying it is your fault is you. Do any of the kids in the school have single mothers?" She nodded and bit her lip. "Have you said to them that it's their fault?" She shook her head again and put her hands over her face. "Would it be fair if someone said that?" She shook her head again. "Well," he said, "since you seem to be able to be fair to them, maybe you should be fair to yourself." That made her cry again but this time the pain didn't last as long.

When she'd wiped her eyes, he said, "Now, how about that Cherry Delight?"

As she pushed him along the sidewalk, she told him about stopping at the artesian well.

"I didn't know it was still flowing," he said. "When I was a boy there was one well at every street corner. I went with a wagon and two pails every day for my mother. I've not tasted water like that in years. It was so cold it could crack your teeth. It had this smooth feeling to it." As he talked about the water, he sat up straighter in the chair and carved the air with his hands.

When he had finished his ice cream, he insisted that she take him to the artesian well.

"It's quite a long way," she said.

"That's all right," he replied.

She'd never seen him like this. She felt that if there was any way that he could walk, he would have got up from the chair and started on his own.

"I haven't had a good drink of water in such a long time. Besides, the walk will do us both good. The doctor says I need to get out into the fresh air. And exercise will help you get over being upset."

As she pushed him, he told her about how in summer he'd sat on the wooden platform that surrounded each pipe and dipped his feet in the water to cool off. In the winter, ice formed into slippery mounds. There was nothing like it, he said, summer or winter, to come to the well and drink your fill.

The streets away from the center of town were quiet. The maple trees hung over the sidewalks, covering them in mottled shade. Many of the yards were surrounded by birch trees. Robins flitted from branch to boulevard.

Frances pushed him over the bridge that spanned the south government ditch. There was only a trickle of water in it. During the summer the grass had grown thick and high. She pushed him along the footpath onto the dirt road.

At last they came to the artesian well. When she arrived, she was thirsty from the heat and the effort of pushing the wheelchair. She crouched beside the pipe, then held her lips against the edge of the stream. She took a mouthful of the icy water and swallowed. The pipe was brown with rust and the wooden platform and the stones where the water fell were stained brown, just as he'd described them being when he was a child.

She realized, as soon as she stepped back, that the wheelchair would not let him close enough to press his lips to the water. She twisted the chair so that he could put his cupped hands under the stream. He tried, but his hands shook with the effort and before he could bring them to his mouth, the water spilled between them.

He tried three times, then shook his head.

"We'd better go," he said. She could hear the disappointment in his voice

"No," she replied. She bent to the well and cupped her hands, filling them with the clear, cold water, then lifted her hands up so that he was able to drink from them. She did this three times for him.

Then he sighed and said, "That's enough."

Suddenly, she burst out, "Sometimes strange things happen to me. Like the other day, I thought I could read Icelandic. I was looking at the words and all of a sudden I understood them. There are other things, too. Do you think I'm crazy?"

"Born under the glacier," he said. "It's like having a

special computer program that allows you to do things other people can't. You can choose to turn it on and use it or not. That's up to you. If you don't use it, it will gradually fade away. At least that's my theory."

"I don't see things the way other kids do."

"Being different is hard," he agreed. "Especially when you are young. Later on it doesn't matter so much." She could see that he was struggling with something. He looked at the sky, then away to the side. "Anyway, I think we should retreat to the coolness of Wrinkle City." Frances's cheeks burned with embarrassment. Mr. J. looked amused. "That's what some people call it, or so I've heard. It's all right. We are all guilty. Every time a teenager goes by, I hear people call them juvenile deliquents."

Back at the library he took a sheaf of papers from his desk.

"I managed to translate quite a bit more. Some of it is impossible. There are pages with no readable date. He pulled a sheet of paper out of his jacket.

"We have taken some land abandoned by Arni Finnson, who has gone to North Dakota. There's a small log cabin. A few stumps have been removed and some of the ground has been cultivated with a mattock. I've planted a few potatoes, beets and turnips but no grain. Pabbi became sick with many others in the immigration shed and the illness keeps returning. We

have a cow. She only has one horn but she gives good milk. I traded my silver filigree belt for three sheep and six chickens. It was my mother's and her mother's before her.

"Then there are pages missing. She either didn't keep a diary for some time or she used more than one book. The next date is three years later. I can't read the day or the month but it says 1891.

"Pabbi's health has worsened. He is now bedridden for most of the day. My aunt complains all the time. She never stops talking about how we should never have left Iceland. She says she only came because she thought we'd have a fine house and beautiful things. We have had to buy groceries on credit at the store and the storekeeper may not allow us to continue. She says if we are going to die of starvation, we might as well have stayed in Iceland.

"Gunnar continues to study in the city. He is very clever with mechanics and has got a job at the gas-works. The hours are long but he says that there is not a great deal to do except check on the dials every so often. It gives him time to study. He writes as often as he can. I don't tell him how things are here because I don't want to distract him from his studies.

"September 25/91. Today, as I was coming from milking, a visitor gave me a fright. It was the under-taker that everyone whispers about. He is tall and

thin. He never said good morning, but stood there
staring at me as I went into our cabin. Then he rudely
pushed open the door and let himself in.

"'Make coffee, Ingibjorg,' my father said. All we have
for coffee is dandelion root but I started the water boil-
ing right away.

"Mr. Soloman never said hello to either Auntie or
me. Instead, he looked around the cabin as if he was
some lord visiting peasants. 'You've no son to help you,'
he said. My aunt bobbed and curtsied and flitted so
much she reminded me of our chicken called Henny.

"After Mr. Soloman left, I asked my father, 'Why did
he come here? There's no one going to die.'

"'He didn't come to measure me for a coffin,' Pabbi
said. 'He's bought up our debts from the storekeeper.
Now he owns us just like he owns everyone else in the
district.'

"November 12/91. Mr. S. came again. We thought it
was to evict us. Instead, he brought us gifts. Coffee for
my father, some black cloth for Auntie and a woolen
shawl for me. After he left, my aunt said, 'His wife died
last year. Now he's a widower.'

"'Do you favor him, Auntie?' I asked.

"'It's not me he's courting,' she said angrily. 'It's not I
who has such fine dark hair.'

"My hand flew to my mouth in surprise. 'But he's
old,' I protested. 'Besides, I'm going to marry Gunnar.'

"'Gunnar will never be able to support you,' my aunt answered. 'Can't you see that your father is getting weaker and weaker? Who knows how much longer he'll live. If you marry wisely, your father will have a fine funeral. He'll be buried in a casket instead of in a pauper's grave.'

"Tonight, I will talk to my grandmother's bones."

"What does that mean?" Frances asked.

"I don't know," Mr. J. said. He rubbed his chin.

"It sounds gross."

Mr. J. had tipped his head back and was looking into the middle distance. When he looked like that, she knew not to interrupt. It meant he was searching for something, a memory or a fact, some faintly remembered clue tucked away years before.

He nodded to himself, then wheeled himself down one of the aisles. When he returned, he had a book on his lap.

"Bones," he said, "aren't always made of bone." He put the book on the table and began to thumb through it.

"There!" Frances exclaimed.

He stopped flipping pages.

"There what?" he said sharply.

"With her dress and her picture. There were sticks with marks like those. Whoops," she added. She'd forgotten that she had meant to keep it a secret.

"Rune staves," he said, looking pleased with himself. She pointed out the ones she recognized. "They're used for casting spells or telling the future. Some people called them the staves of the weird. She probably cast the staves onto a white cloth to read the future. Or she may have cast a spell to protect her father from illness. There were lots of spells. Brun-runa was to make the lake calm instead of stormy. Bjorg-runa was to help a woman give birth easily."

"Runa," Frances said. "That was her middle name. The person who knows. If she could do these things, why is it such a big secret?"

"If she did, it was not something to talk about. The church banned the runes as witchcraft. In 1681 a man called Arni Petursson was burned alive in the presence of the Icelandic Althing for using runic talismans while gambling at backgammon. I think we should stick with the diary."

"But it's interesting," Frances said.

"I'm not sure your mother would approve."

"My mother doesn't approve of anything Icelandic. She's always saying things like, 'What do you want to wear an Icelandic sweater for when you can get real British woolens?' You'd think she was born in Marks and Spencer."

She could see that he was torn, looking at her, then

back at the manuscript. Finally, the manuscript won. He started to read.

"December 20/91. The winter has hardened. The cow has quit giving milk. Our chickens lay few eggs. We've been living on dried fish and potatoes. My father is too ill to go into the bush and cut firewood to sell. Today, when I was in the barn, one of the boys I saw on the boat came. His name is...

"The ink has hardened and rubbed off in places so all I get is a word or two," Mr. J. complained. "It's very frustrating. Here is Gunnar's name." He used his finger to show Frances on the paper. "This says *visit.* But the way it is written means *will come to visit.* I can't make anything out of this." He ran his finger down the page. "This says *ham and potatoes, rice and raisins.* But whether they've bought them or Gunnar brought them, I don't know. This next sentence is complete. It says, *I've not had raisins since we left Iceland.* Then *My father.* I think this says *tobacco, my aunt a bottle of sherry.* Then I can't read it until it says *my hair. I did not want it but took it because I was afraid to offend him. Before he left, he invited us to come and stay with him over Christmas."*

He stopped reading and asked, "What do you know about the Jolasvenir?"

"Christmas weiners?"

Mr. J. laughed out loud. "No, not Christmas weiners. The Christmas boys. The Yule boys."

"Nothing," she said but, as she said it, she felt it wasn't true. Images briefly appeared, overlapping, voices, confusion. "At least, I don't think so."

"They're folklore," Mr. J. said. "There are thirteen of them. The first one comes thirteen days before Christmas. After that one appears each day. They have names like Skyr Gobbler, Pot Licker, Door Slammer."

Frances didn't know what to answer. The discussion had stirred up feelings that swirled inside her like rapidly moving colors. Quickly she changed the subject.

"Gunnar couldn't have brought gifts like that. He had no money. Besides, she would have been happy with anything Gunnar gave her. Mr. S. has come to visit again," Frances said. She could feel her temper flaring up. "The aunt is wrong. She's trying to make Ingibjorg marry someone she doesn't love."

17

....
....

Frances went to the library to borrow a book on runes, then rode her bike out of town on the northern section of the pioneer highway. The town graveyard was just beyond where it met the main highway there.

Like most prairie graveyards, there was nothing fancy about it. A white fence surrounded it. At the front there was a wrought-iron gate.

Frances propped her bike against the fence and climbed through the railings. She'd been past the graveyard many times but had never been inside. She thought there might be a map showing where people were buried but there wasn't, so she decided to be methodical and walk up and down the rows.

She started on the south side and worked her way to the north side. She had intended to make a quick check, but then she recognized the names on some of the tombstones and realized they were from families she knew. Some of the older graves were of children. She stopped to wonder about them. Mr. J. said there weren't medicines then like there were now. He'd told her about whole families dying from measles. "Everybody's always talking about the good old days," he said. "Count your blessings."

She was halfway when she stopped with a shock. There was a white headstone. The lettering was worn from the weather but it clearly said *Thorbjorg Johannson and infant daughter, Iris. Never to be forgotten.* Frost had tipped the stone slightly.

A short distance away she came across the graves of her great-grandparents, Lauga and Herman. They had been Fjola's parents.

She thought about the chart she was making. She had a picture of them taken on their wedding day. Lauga was wearing a huge hat with flowers on it and Herman looked like he could barely breathe in his three-piece suit.

She thought she'd find Ingibjorg and Gunnar close by, but there was no sign of their graves. She walked along all the rows. Some graves were unmarked. She knew they were graves because the ground was sunken slightly.

As she searched, cars zipped by on the highway. Rushing here, rushing there. Every so often there'd be a blast of music from one of them, then the sound would fade. Behind her was the new golf course. It had been one of the early settler's farms. There were birds circling high above. She wondered if they were ravens or crows. Keeping an eye on me, she thought, then laughed.

When she got home, her gran and her mother were sitting in the living room. They'd obviously been talking about her because they stopped as she came in the door.

She was going to go straight to her bedroom when her mother said, "Frances. We need to talk to you."

Reluctantly, she sat down on the edge of a chair.

"There's still room on the charter your grandmother is taking to Iceland," her mother said. "If you want to go, I'll pay for your fare. If you want to see your father, I'll call him. You don't have to see him, of course. He wouldn't have to know that you were there."

"Why would he want to see me now when he never wanted to see me before?" she said bitterly.

"At first his wife didn't know. Then he told her. After that he wrote. He wanted to correspond with you. I told him no."

She wondered if she was supposed to be happy about this.

"That's what you wanted. What about me?" she asked.

"You were a baby. You can't ask a baby, can you? Maybe you're right. Maybe that's just what I wanted and I didn't think it through. But I'm human, too. Everything was fine until he came along and then he left everybody else to deal with the consequences. Me, you, your grandparents. I just wanted to forget he'd ever been here."

For a moment, Frances saw her mother's carefully managed mask crumple. There was the voice and face of someone much younger who sounded hurt and confused.

"I've taken care of us. We weren't going to be a burden on anyone."

"We never thought you were a burden, Emily," Gran said. "Neither you, nor Frances. When you love someone, they are never a burden."

"Has he any kids?" Frances asked to fill the silence.

"Three. One boy and a girl are quite a bit older than you. Jon is married and has a son. Katrina is eighteen. Harldur is about two months older than you. You've always said you wanted brothers and sisters."

"Maybe," Frances said. If there had been an earthquake and a chasm had opened up and swallowed her, she wouldn't have been surprised. "Maybe not. I'm not sure. I'll have to think about it."

"We have to book tickets by next Wednesday. You've got six days to think about it."

Her mother tugged at her blouse and pushed at her hair the way someone might before they went on stage, except that it didn't help. Emotions kept sweeping over her like gusts of wind over the surface of the lake.

"Sure," Frances replied. "I'll think about it."

There was nothing better than fishing to help her think. She was putting bait on her hooks when her gran joined her.

"She's pretty upset," she said.

"What about me?" Frances replied. "I noticed that she knows about his family. Everybody in town knows about him and her and me. There's that stupid Frances, she doesn't even know…"

She stopped. If she kept on, she was going to start yelling or crying.

"I'm the only one left in the dark." She cast so hard that both minnows came off the hooks. She started to reel her line back in.

"He didn't know that his wife was pregnant until he got back. That's why his youngest is just about the same age as you."

"He's a jerk," Frances said.

"I guess," Gran said, handing her two minnows. "Most of us do jerky things now and again. But if I could change what happened, would I? Not if it meant that I didn't get to drag for minnows with you or go bike riding with you. Your grandpa Villy wouldn't have traded you for anything. You may not remember it, but he carted you everywhere. When you were three, you used to stand on the tailgate of his truck and sing. You were a real ham."

"I visited the graveyard today," Frances said. "I saw Grandma Lauga and Grandpa Herman and Grandpa Villy's graves. I thought Ingibjorg and Gunnar would be there, too."

"Gunnar wanted to be buried close to the lake. His grave was north of here at Kirkjabaer. Ingibjorg wanted to be buried where he was."

"Can we go there?" Frances asked.

"Yes," Gran said, "but there won't be anything to see. There were a number of years of high water and all the graves close to the shore were washed away."

Frances's hand closed more tightly about the rod. She remembered from the diary that Ingibjorg's greatest fear had been being buried at sea.

For a moment, it was as if she were no longer standing on the sand, as if she didn't exist except for sound and feeling, as if she were bones washing back and forth with the action of the waves. The sound roared in her ears the way it did when she dove from the dock into the lake. Gradually it faded and she was back again, holding the rod, staring across the water.

"How come Mr. J. has no family? Nobody ever comes to visit him. When I was at the graveyard today, I saw a grave for a mother and baby. It had the same last name on the stone."

"He was in Europe in the war. They got the flu. Lots of people died."

"He never said."

"Did you ask?"

She hadn't, she realized. When she visited him, it was to find out about her great-greats. She went to see him because he could read Icelandic, not to hear his life story.

She started to feel uncomfortable and changed the subject.

"Was she a witch?"

"Who? Grandma Ingibjorg? Worse. She was a Lutheran. I'll take witches any time. They're a lot more fun. She was hell on wheels in the Ladies Aid. She ran that kitchen like a master sargeant. Make those sandwiches. Serve that coffee."

"I'm serious," Frances said. "She was into herbs and things."

"I give you echinacea when you get a cold. Does that make me a witch?"

"How did the house burn down?"

"You're like a dog after a bone. If this keeps up, you'll become a prosecutor feared by criminals far and wide. The house was struck by lightning. It had a widow's walk. That's a metal fence. Everything here is flat. Lake, sandbar, lagoon. The house must have been the highest thing around for miles. I don't know why the guy who built it didn't just attach a metal rod to his head and stand out in a storm. Totally dumb. There's probably a deep and profound moral if you just look hard enough. Vanity creates its own destruction or something. He should have planted birches around it. Look, your great-great was an amazing woman. She made friends with the native people. They knew they could stop at the farm any time, night or day. In return they taught her things like what tree bark to brew to stop diarrhea."

"Why birches?"

"They are sacred to Thor. He's the god of thunder and birches will protect a house from thunder and lightning. At least that's the theory."

"Ginger snaps," Frances replied. "There's bank robberies and you talk ginger snaps. There's more to the birches. There's stuff you're not saying. I just know it."

"You know something? She was ahead of her time. If she was alive now, she'd be running a health food store and practicing all this New Age stuff with crystals and acupuncture and aromatherapy. Now, if you don't go to town and buy the stuff on this grocery list, we're not going to have supper. Be sure to get the eggs that are on sale."

She was putting groceries into her saddlebags when Wendy came over from the post office. She had been mailing some letters. "My mom says you've taken to swimming in the ditch."

"I fell off my bike. I was racing your brother."

"Speaking of my brother," Wendy said, "I see that you're wearing the ring he gave you."

Frances looked down at Wendy's hand. "So are you. So what?"

"I think he thinks you're an item."

"Did he say that?"

"No. But I saw the hug you gave him the other day. Besides, he's always tagging along when I come to see you. What do you think? He's babysitting?"

Frances felt a sense of shock. Bryan! Coming around because of her. Not because he had nothing better to do. Turning up unexpectedly here and there, just casual like. She had a boyfriend and didn't even know it.

Dumb, dumb, dumb, she said to herself. Can't see what's in front of your face. She thought about how she had climbed on his shoulders and suddenly felt embarrassed. Sherlock Holmes would have spotted all the evidence in a glance. She prided herself on seeing things and missed the most obvious. The Purloined Letter all over again.

She left early the next morning, slipping out to avoid everyone—her amma, her mother, Bryan. She didn't want any distractions.

She usually met with Mr. J. at two o'clock. She wondered if it would be all right to arrive early.

She fished at the dock, then gave her two pickerel to a kid who wasn't catching anything because he never set his hook properly. At eleven o'clock she went to the OFH and asked for Mr. J. This time Whitey smiled and told her to try the library.

When she went in, he had the pages of the diary spread out on the table.

"I haven't been able to do much," he said. "My eyes are bothering me."

"Yesterday evening, Mr. S. came for us. My father lay in the back of the sleigh covered in buffalo robes. My aunt sat up front with Mr. S. It was not so long a ride before I could see the lights of Mr. S.'s house. He left us at the door, then continued on to town to take Father to see a doctor. The woman servant who acts as both cook and maid showed us to our rooms where I fell asleep at once. This morning Mr. S. said my father had taken a turn for the worse so he had arranged for him to be taken to Selkirk by a freighter that was hauling fish. We had breakfast in the dining room. I have never seen food like this, not in Iceland, not in Canada. There were two kinds of bread, jars of

jam, rich cream, boiled eggs, ham, fried potatoes.

"'This is a fine house,' my aunt said, feeling the drapes. 'And fine furnishings. And fine food. There is everything that anyone could want to be happy.'

"After breakfast, Mr. S. led me up a narrow set of stairs through the attic. He opened a trap door so we could climb onto the roof. There was a flat area enclosed by a black metal fence. From where we stood, I could see across the marsh all the way to where the trees marked its eastern perimeter. It was a white wasteland of ice and snow. The snow drifted across it in waves.

"'All this will be yours,' he said, flinging out his long, skinny arm. 'I know I'm not young but young men are usually poor and who knows if they will ever be anything else?'

"This evening, my aunt entertained us by playing the piano. When Mr. S. went to get us coffee, she hissed, 'See this fine piano? If you were mistress of this house, I could play it for you every day.'

"That is all," Mr. J. said. "Oh, to be seventy again. You and I, Frances, would be a great team. And your friend, what's his name, could take photographs. We could tell lots of stories."

"Was there nothing more about runes?" she asked.

"Nothing but that one mention. Remember that many pages are still missing."

She showed him the book of runes. "I've been reading about rune casting."

"There are risks," he said. "There are things that should be left alone."

She hesitated, unsure of how to put it. "I went to the graveyard. I saw your family."

He looked surprised. "I haven't been there in a long time. A wheelchair doesn't do too well on a gravel road and the highway's a bit dangerous."

"My gran would take you," Frances said, then remembered she shouldn't be volunteering someone else for something. She hated it when her mother did that to her. "I'll ask her."

"I should be polite and say, oh, no, that would be too much trouble, but I'm too old for that. If she'd drive me, I'd like to take some irises. My wife loved irises. They were the same color as her eyes."

"Sure," Frances said. There was a long silence. "Do you know about the graveyard north of here that got washed away?"

"Yes," he answered. "Not all of it. But twenty feet or so. They've put a breakwater in since."

"My great-greats were there."

"These things happen," he said. "Why don't we cheer up with some coffee and cake? If we keep this up, we'll have little black clouds floating over our heads."

When she left, she went to the school grounds. Craig and Roger were shooting baskets. Wendy was standing on the sidelines watching.

Craig threw Frances the ball. She dribbled it to get the feel right, then threw. The ball came off the backboard. Right away both boys were making comments about some people losing their touch. She dropped the next one through the net and took the third one off the backboard.

Three more kids she didn't recognize stopped by. She didn't know their names but they wanted to play three on three.

It's good, she thought, to do something sometimes where you are just thinking about right now.

18

"'If we're to prosper in this new land,' Mr. S. said as he ate his sausages, 'we have to be practical.' He'd arranged for my aunt to eat in the sunroom so that we could be alone. 'I came to America with hardly a penny in my pocket. Now I have all this. Why? Because I was practical. I could have been a farmer but everything is unpredictable. The weather, the price for crops, the cost of seed. I could have been a fisherman but I asked myself, what is guaranteed in life? Death. Everyone will be my customer some day.

"'Your father needs medical attention. Everything you own is mortgaged. If the mortgage holder forecloses, where will you go? You might get work as a domestic in Winnipeg but what of your aunt? What of your father? Look around you. I have things that no one else has. Beautiful things.'

"As I sat there, I prayed that the boys would remember to help me.

"The next pages are too faded. They look like they were left in the sun. Anyway, we know it came out all right in the end. I found some more about Gunnar in a book written by Fridrik Fridjonsson. He says that Gunnar traveled all over the district teaching people in their homes. He even went on snowshoes in winter. Many of the people couldn't pay. Sometimes they'd give him fish or eggs, whatever they had. One family gave him a deerskin jacket. Later, he had a one-room school of his own."

As Mr. J. spoke, Frances felt like she was standing on a grassy point of land looking over a vast expanse of snow and forest. On the horizon was the far shore. A figure on snowshoes was moving toward her over the snowdrifts.

Seeing in images is a bit like dreaming, she realized, but it's also another way of thinking.

"I'm going to use it," she said.

"Use what?" Mr. J. asked, confused.

"Being born under the glacier." She couldn't think how to explain it logically but then an image came sweeping in. "It's like I see a rainbow just like everybody else sees a rainbow but there's color on either side of the rainbow that most people don't see." She hesitated. "That isn't all of it. It's like feeling the rainbow. People will think I'm weird."

"Don't tell them. Don't waste time arguing about

whether there are colors on the edge of the rainbow. They see their way. You see yours."

Mrs. Thorlaksson, one of the ladies who lived in the home, came to say that their bridge game was ready to start.

"What should I bid?" Mr. J. said to Frances jokingly.

"Three no trump," Frances replied. She knew that three no trump was Mr. J.'s favorite bid. Other kids were playing with dolls when she was learning how to sluff a card.

That was the problem with being an only child, her gran had said on more than one occasion. You ended up learning how to do adult things long before you should. She wondered whether she'd be more normal if her dad and mom had done things normally. Like having tea parties with other kids instead of with her imaginary playmates.

Later, when Frances returned, she found Mr. J. in the library.

"I can't make anything out of what's left," he said. "I'm sorry." He asked her to take him to the monument built to commemorate the first settlers. It was made from granite beach stone, large rocks that were pink and gray. Sunlight flashed and winked from the bits of mica embedded in the stone. On top was a massive rock.

Frances pushed him down the street to the park and the pavilion.

"There used to be a forest of magnificent spruce trees here. There was a terrible storm in '45. Spruce are shallow rooted and most of them toppled. Everything changes. You can't cut down the forest and then expect isolated groups of trees to stay standing. One change causes another."

He handed her a barley sugar. He was addicted to it in spite of the fact that he was supposed to limit the amount of sugar he ate. Between the ice-cream cones and the candy, she expected that he was going to succumb to a sugar fit one of these days.

The door to the pavilion was open and there were boards forming a ramp on the stairs. He got her to push him up. It was an old-fashioned dance hall with the floor enclosed by beams and half walls. An interior walkway went all the way around.

"Stop," he said when they were halfway round. "Right here is where I met my wife. She was sitting on one of those benches. Probably the same benches. I was standing over here trying to work up enough nerve to ask her to dance when they called a lady's choice. She came right up and asked me to do a waltz. That's the way she was. No pussyfooting."

Pussyfooting. It had a nice sound to it. Quit that pussyfooting.

They went around another corner. There was a man with a bright red face stacking chairs.

"I see you've got an assistant," he said to Mr. J.

"That's right, Joe. And there isn't a better one anywhere. This here's Frances, Emily's daughter. Fjola and Villy's granddaughter." Joe shook her hand.

After they were out of the hall, Mr. J. said, "You see that Joe? High blood pressure's going to kill him one of these days. He should have retired years ago. He's just the caretaker. Not much of a story there to look at him. Except you catch him having coffee some day when he's not busy. You ask him how he liked his visit to Korea. Maybe he'll tell why he always sets off the metal detectors at the airport."

Frances made a note in her notebook. She was creating a list of possible articles.

"Is there nothing more you know about my great-great?" Frances asked. She felt a great hollow inside. There was something she needed to know but she didn't know what it was.

"Not much," Mr. J. said. "No facts."

"What about non-facts? Are there any of those?" She was wondering if her gran had learned to talk about ginger snaps from him.

"Stories, rumors, gossip, lies, half-truths, speculation. Not the sort of thing a responsible person would give any credence to."

"Sometimes a bit of gossip is like a thread that leads to something big unraveling." That wasn't quite how her gran had put it but it seemed close.

She could see he was struggling over what to tell her or whether to tell her anything at all.

"Seven no trump," she said, challenging him to risk everything with the biggest bid possible in bridge.

"Doubled," he said.

"Redoubled."

"You're a real risk-taker. All right. Mr. Soloman and the aunt disappeared. I've heard the story a number of different ways. Things get embellished. There was a Christmas Eve party. A lot of people came. Mr. Soloman may have hoped to celebrate his betrothal to Ingibjorg. At eleven o'clock there was to be a huge feast, but when the doors were opened, there was nothing on the table but empty plates and bottles. The entire meal had been eaten. Only the Yule boys could have done that. It would take all thirteen of them but they weren't called names like Spoon Licker, Ham Snitcher and Skyr Gobbler for nothing."

"Do you believe any of this?" Frances asked.

"There are stranger things in this world than science has any answer for," Mr. J. said. "I have no doubt about some of it."

"The foundation of the house exists. I found it."

"Everyone was terribly poor. The poor resent the rich. They love stories about the poor getting the better of the rich. They have so little real power that they often invoke supernatural assistance."

"The Yule boys," Frances said. "The boys on the ship." She shut her eyes for a moment. Sudden, faded images of boys laughing, chasing her, playing tag around the farm, climbing trees, swinging on the swing and sharing her lemonade swirled in her head, then were gone.

"After everyone left, Mr. Soloman was furious. Ingibjorg's aunt was very materialistic and snobbish. She was described as always putting on airs, even when her skirts were patched. She wasn't well liked." Frances said she understood. "Her aunt was going to lock Ingibjorg out in the cold until she agreed to marry Mr. Soloman. Somehow, Ingibjorg reversed the situation and locked them out. Mr. Soloman kept his horse and sleigh in a shed at the back. He and the aunt started across the bay for town. A terrible blizzard came up. For days afterward people searched for them but it was like they'd simply vanished. They probably got turned around in the snow, stopped and got drifted over. In the spring, everything would have sunk into the lake.

"Some people said they'd eloped. Since he couldn't have the daughter, he'd have the aunt. They thought they'd traveled to Selkirk and taken the train. There were lots of stories. People kept seeing them here and there but nothing ever came of it. They never returned."

"Did Ingibjorg stay in the house?"

"Yes. For three years. Her father came back and lived with her. He gradually became well enough to work again."

"Why is it such a big secret?"

Mr. J. cleared his throat. "Some said she'd killed them and buried the bodies. But it was impossible. It was the dead of winter. The ground was as hard as iron. Some said she used magic. Her family—your family—had a certain reputation in Iceland. They were Christians but they followed the old religion, too. Mind you, they drank no horse blood, made no sacrifices."

"Some people thought she'd killed them?"

"Superstition. Ignorance. Jealousy. When the house was struck by lightning, some said it was a sign."

"What do you think?"

"I think that Mr. Soloman and the aunt were not very nice people. Ingibjorg was a young girl. Unless you think she gave them forty whacks, then carved them up and ate them, I'd go with getting lost in the storm."

They had stopped at the end of the road. The pale yellow beach was before them and, beyond that, the silver lake.

Frances felt a kind of happy confusion. Turmoil, she thought, but not wild turmoil. More like when a bunch of relatives came that they hadn't seen in a long time. All saying hello and shaking hands and everyone talking at once.

Beside them was a mountain ash. She turned Mr. J.'s chair to face it.

"We have those at the farm," she said.

"A fine tree. Very decorative in winter with their red berries."

"They have another name."

"Is that so?" When he didn't want to tell her something he always let his voice go flat and his face became unexpressive.

"It's called a rowan tree."

"Fancy that," he said.

"It's also known as the tree of runes. It can be used against black magic and bad luck."

"There are lots of them in Iceland."

"I thought there were no trees in Iceland."

"The countryside was covered in trees when it was settled. The settlers used the trees for fuel and building. The sheep did the rest. Still, trees do grow if the sheep are kept away."

When he was like this, she felt so frustrated she wanted to stamp her feet and yell.

"Why do you keep hiding things about the runes?" She didn't mean to sound so angry but she could hear the sharpness in her voice.

"This is nothing to fool around with," he said. "There are paths that it is dangerous to go down. We start innocently enough. Then we begin to know things. It is better for most people not to know. Learn about your ancestors, fine. I said I'd help you with that."

"They're from a long time ago. It's all in the past."

"Do you think that?" he said sharply. "Look around you. The Futhark is everywhere. It's just that people have lost the ability to see." He pointed at two twigs crossed on the ground. "There is Gebo." He stabbed his finger at a cut branch that looked like a Y with the center stem continued. "There is Elhaz. Here is Ansuz." He pointed to a crack in the clay that looked like a slanted capital F. "Because people cannot see does not mean that there is nothing to be seen."

She wondered, listening to him, if this was what her gran had meant when she had said skeletons can dance. The past seemed vague and distant, a few words and pictures on a page. History was of no importance to your life until you began to learn about it, and then it was all around you, influencing everything you did.

She took him back to the OFH. She and her gran were going to come in two days to take him out to the graveyard. Afterwards they were going to take a drive along the lake so he could see the old farmsteads. Then they were going to go for lunch at a restaurant. Her gran said that was for the A plus he'd given her on one of her exams.

Gran was in town shopping. Frances joined her. As they rode back on their bikes, Frances told her Mr. J.'s story of the house.

"She didn't own the property," her gran said. "She stayed because the house would have been empty and her father needed a place better than the cabin. When it burned down, she saved some things. I don't know what happened to them. Your grandfather bought the property for back taxes. I think I remember him saying that it cost him fifty dollars. No one wanted to live so far out of town in those days. Now I wish he'd bought the whole island."

Her gran spent the rest of the day making plans for a blockade of the road. There was just the one road in and it was narrow and it would be easy to stop traffic. A dozen grandmothers in long dresses and funny hats lying on it would stop just about anything. Emily was off showing a waterfront listing that was going to pay for the trip to Iceland—if Frances decided to go.

˙ All that digging and all she'd really discovered was that she had a dad and a family that was even stranger than she'd imagined. And now she had secrets of her own. Being a detective didn't seem like such a great idea anymore.

She didn't sleep much that night. The next morning, early, she went to town and found her Barbie tea set in the shed. She put it in her pack. She wrapped up a dozen of Gran's chocolate chip cookies and filled a thermos with lemonade.

She bumped into Bryan as she was leaving. He offered to come with her. She told him that she had something that she had to do by herself but she wouldn't mind going canoeing later. She wondered if he knew about her dad. It seemed like everyone in the community knew except her. Maybe that's why Mrs. Skillings acted so superior.

She rode out to the farm and propped her bike up against the farmhouse wall. Then she used a metal bar from the farm machinery to pry the boards off the front door. She pried the ladder off the barn wall. It just reached the pantry ceiling.

She climbed up and went to the fish box and took out her great-great's dress. She took the runes and from beneath them the faded red pillow embroidered with runic signs. That, she now knew from her reading, was the stol. Beneath that was the large white cloth. This had to be Ingibjorg's casting cloth. It was to be as tall as the person casting the runes when she had her arms held up and as wide as when she had her arms held out. Frances held up the sheet and found it was the right length. Then she held out her arms and found it was the right width.

Finally, there was a small cloth. A personal talisman was to be placed upon it.

She played the flashlight over the attic. Her light showed some white and black feathers. She took one of each color.

She took everything to the log cabin. This is where she and her imaginary friends used to have their tea parties. When the cups and plates were set out, she poured the lemonade.

She thought they might reappear like real boys and sit down and be jolly and joking the way they had when she was little, but it wasn't like that anymore. She knew they were there but they seemed to form and dissolve the way a daydream does.

If anyone had come then, all they would have seen, of course, was Frances having a tea party with a little kid's dishes. That crazy Sigurdsson girl is at it again, they'd have said. But she didn't care. She wanted the boys to know that she appreciated the fact that, somehow, they had been there for Ingibjorg when she needed them and they'd been there when she needed them.

She laid the casting cloth on the ground. She remembered what she had read. The caster was to place herself in the face of the sun, in the eye of the light. Then she placed the small white cloth on top of the casting cloth and placed both the black feather and the white on it.

When all was done, she sat on the pillow with the runes in her hands. The book had emphasized, time and again, that the caster must not ask a question when it is rainy or cloudy or windy or when you are angry or when your mind is thinking of other things or when there are skeptics near.

She was angry, she realized. Angry with her mother. Angry with her father. Angry with her grandmother. Her anger was like a red dust devil twirling furiously inside her.

But she wanted to ask, and the wanting was greater than the anger.

She remembered her gran teaching her to relax by breathing with her stomach instead of her chest. She took a deep breath and let her stomach rise.

She thought about all the good things her mother and grandmother had done. She said to herself that she forgave her father. She repeated it again and again until the dust devil grew smaller and smaller and spun itself out of existence. Knowing was more important than being angry.

The silence was so complete that she could hear her heart beating.

Without meaning to, she passed the runes from one hand to the other. She remembered the static crackle that had filled her head when she'd asked a question of Huginn and Muninn. Mr. J. had said the ravens spoke in runes. It was a speech long forgotten. Ravens and people no longer spoke the same language.

She passed the runes back, then back again. The question had to be absolutely clear. "Am I to go to Iceland?" she whispered and cast the runes.

When she looked, many of the runes had fallen face down but the two closest to her, lying beside each other, were Raido and Enwaz. As a diad they meant a journey.

Frances listened to the silence that filled up everything. Gradually sound began to filter in. She looked around. Everything was as it had been—the house, the barn, the log cabin, the fields, the wildflowers, the sound of traffic in the distance. Carefully, she picked up the runes. She left the cookies for the boys. Then she folded up the two cloths, piled everything on the pillow and took it all back to the attic.

She left the box and its contents. It was too much

right now to take it home. It would mean having to deal with her mother and gran. Later, when she came back from Iceland, she'd "discover" it. She was also going to call her mother Mom from now on. Whether she liked it or not.

Frances hung around the house the next day, talking to Gran about the trip, looking at brochures. What clothes she should take. Where they should go. Gran wanted to rent a car and drive right around the island. Frances wanted to swim in the Blue Lagoon and climb on a glacier. They both agreed that their first priority was to visit the farms where the great-greats had come from. The question about whether she would see her father was left unanswered. That she would decide for herself.

The day after that they went to pick up Mr. J., but he wasn't on the front porch waiting for them. Frances looked in the dining room. Then she went to the front desk. Mrs. Arnason said they'd taken him to the hospital. Frances wasn't sure how she turned into Mrs. Arnason from Whitey. Probably the way she told her about Mr. J.

He'd been having chest pains. Before he left, he gave her something for Frances. Frances thought it was going to be the diary. Instead, it was an envelope and inside there was a gift certificate for thirty-five ice-cream cones. On the back of the certificate was the sentence, "The farm's original name was Hrafna Heimili. Raven's home. Not Midas. Change the sign."

Gran drove Frances to the hospital. She asked to see Mr. J. but the receptionist said he'd had a stroke and wouldn't know she was there. Frances said that was okay.

The room was white and there were three other beds. She pulled the screen so that they'd have some privacy. She sat beside the bed for awhile, then quietly told him that she was going to Iceland. She'd read somewhere that even when people are in comas, they can hear what someone says. She held his hand and said thanks for the gift certificate and the translations and everything. Then she went outside where it was like nothing had happened. The highway was jammed with tourists rushing back to the city.

The next day she went to the OFH and explained to Mrs. Arnason about the diary. She checked his room but it wasn't there. She suggested that Frances look in the library. Frances went over the shelves and even through the desk. It wasn't there.

It was just a bunch of cut-up, moldy, mouse-eaten paper in a language she couldn't read, but she wanted it more than nearly anything. She wanted one day to be able to read it for herself.

She checked her pocket. She had six dollars. She went to the florist. She put her six dollars on the counter and explained why she wanted flowers. The florist, like everyone else in town, was a cousin of sorts, and she gave Frances a special deal that included a vase for holding water so the irises wouldn't wilt right away. She threw in a few more irises for the same price. That was because the florist's mom had had Mr. J. for a teacher.

Frances took the flowers out to the graveyard.

"This is from Mr. J.," she said and put the flowers in front of the headstone. "He can't make it."

When she stood up, she saw a long white line in the sky. By shielding her eyes, she could just barely see the plane. It was going somewhere—maybe New York, maybe London, maybe Iceland. Mr. J. had said use the past as a compass to navigate the future but live in the present.

Being born under a glacier wasn't such a bad thing. She saw the glare of ice, heard the steady pounding of waves on a lava shore, tasted salt air.

That's where she was going. Her ticket was for one but, she thought, it was a deal because she was taking a crowd with her.